MIGHTIER

THAN THE

SWORD

THE EDGE OF THE WORD

PENGUIN WORKSHOP
An Imprint of Penguin Random House LLC, New York

Penguin supports copyright. Copyright fuels creativity, encourages diverse voices, promotes free speech, and creates a vibrant culture. Thank you for buying an authorized edition of this book and for complying with copyright laws by not reproducing, scanning, or distributing any part of it in any form without permission. You are supporting writers and allowing Penguin to continue to publish books for every reader.

Text copyright © 2019 by Drew Callander and Alana Harrison. Illustrations copyright © 2019 by Ryan Andrews. All rights reserved. Published by Penguin Workshop, an imprint of Penguin Random House LLC, New York. PENGUIN and PENGUIN WORKSHOP are trademarks of Penguin Books Ltd, and the W colophon is a registered trademark of Penguin Random House LLC. Printed in the USA.

Visit us online at www.penguinrandomhouse.com.

Library of Congress Cataloging-in-Publication Data is available upon request.

ISBN 9781524785109   10 9 8 7 6 5 4 3 2 1

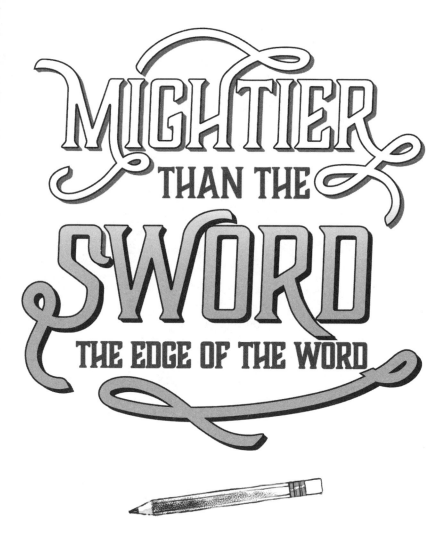

MIGHTIER THAN THE SWORD

THE EDGE OF THE WORD

DREW CALLANDER & ALANA HARRISON

ART BY RYAN ANDREWS AND YOU!

Penguin Workshop

For Chuck and Holly—you were always home to us.
—DC & AH

For Alex—RA

Every one is a moon, and has a dark side
which he never shows to anybody.
—Mark Twain, "Pudd'nhead Wilson's New Calendar,"
Following the Equator

A Note to the Reader

This book is unlike any book you've ever read before. Unless you've read the previous book, *Mightier Than the Sword*. Then you've read one book like this before, and you already know that unlike regular books that tell you about other people, this book tells you about you.

Yes, you.

While it's true that you're safely on Earth reading these very words right now, it's also true that you've somehow gotten yourself stranded in a strange world a bazillion light-years away.

How can you be in two places at once? Good question! We'd like to know, too, but we aren't privy[1] to that information.

---

1 "Privy" means knowing something that is otherwise secret or hidden, which is often the way we use these footnotes, to make you privy to a little more information that you wouldn't otherwise have known (like that "privy" is also a word for an outdoor toilet [strange, because using an outdoor toilet is probably not an easy thing to keep secret]).

What we do know is that you need your help. You may not survive this adventure without it. Thanks to a serious case of amnesia, you don't even know your name. But, over the last twelve hours, you have managed to learn a few things:

1) You're a real human being. (This may not sound like much of a discovery, but it is when you consider the following.)

2) You're in a fictional world. It's called Astorya, and it's where stories written by real human beings come to life.

3) You have a pencil. An ordinary pencil from the real world. This makes it extraordinary in Astorya.

4) Since you are a real human being in a fictional world, anything you write with your real pencil will spring into full-fledged fictional existence. This makes you kind of a superhero.

5) You created this fictional world. You did it by writing the original *A Story of Astorya*.[2] This makes you kind of a god.

---

2 Technically, you haven't written it yet. But you're going to write it. Someday. And then it will arrive in Astorya in the past. The distant past. So far back that it will arrive on the very first day.

Congratulations! You're nearing superhero-god status, and all you had to do was read 384 words.

But you're not one of those immortal superhero-gods. You're still a real human being. That means you face real consequences, despite being in a fictional world. And this fictional world can be quite dangerous for a real human being like you. Fatal, even.

We know this is all pretty heavy for just 438 words into a story. But it's not so bad. You survived the first book, defeated the evil Queen Rulette and her hordes of Rubot minions, saved the world, and earned the respect and friendship of the Couriers, the sworn protectors of Astorya. You didn't make it back to Earth, but hey, that's what sequels are for.

So grab your pencil—you'll need it if you ever want to make it home in one piece.

CHAPTER ONE

"What a nightmare," whispers Manteau. Your little stoat friend sits on your shoulder. His black, beady eyes remain fixed on where the Fuchsia Plum Palace towered less than an hour ago. In its place swirls a vast gray smudge. From where you stand atop the GPS,[3] you can see the entire sprawl of erasure it left behind.

"I know," you say to your furry companion. Nightmare. That sums it up pretty well. You think of all that Queen Rulette forced you to endure. Her poofy attack poodles, her creepy portraits, her cake-filled party pit, her horrible singing, her dungeon slick with despair, her

---

3 Giant Poop Ship. In case you forgot, the Couriers' ship is a giant ball of poo. Don't blame us, *you* wrote it.

groveling lapdog Fwoofwoo, her fake laugh and thick makeup, and, of course, her legions of ruthless Rubots. Your leg still throbs from where one of them singed you with its fuchsia-plum laser.

"But at least it's over," you tell Manteau, shifting your weight off your injured leg. Rulette may have stolen your ride home, but thanks to you, she won't be giving Astorya any more trouble. You can't stop a smile from spreading across your lips. Against all odds, you saved the world.

"What?" he snaps. "Zee nightmare isn't over! It's right there!"

You realize the nightmare Manteau refers to isn't Rulette, but the erasure you made when you erased her story. For the fictional, like your furry friend, erasure is death.

"I know you had no choice," he says, "but just look at zat . . ." His little body shudders. "*Quelle horreur!*[4] How could you?!"

"How could I?" you say, stung by his question. "Don't you remember what she did to you?"

"Don't remind me," Manteau says. "You are zee one wiz zee bad memory. Not *moi*."

---

4 As Manteau is French, he sometimes speaks French. To clarify when he is speaking French, the words are in *italics*. You can find out what they mean by turning to page 328, "Not Enough French to Speak French, but Enough to Sound Like Maybe You Know How."

"She erased you!" you say.

"I told you not to remind me!" he says.

"She was going to erase everything! Everyone! All of Astoria!"

"I know! I know!" he says, throwing his paws up in the air. "Rulette was a fiend and a coward! I'm glad she's gone. Good riddance!"

"And . . . ?"

"And I, of course, am eternally grateful to you for writing me back to life. Zat goes wizout saying, *non*? You don't need to rub it in! You don't hear me rubbing it in about all zee times I saved your life, do you?"

"What do you mean 'all the times'?" You only recall that one instance when he saved you from the Dust Bunnies.

"*Exactement!* You don't hear me doing it!" He heaves out a sigh and looks at the erasure. "It's just, *zut alors*, look at what you've done!"

You stare at the erasure. It seethes like a fresh wound, demanding attention. Its hurried, jagged edges bully the world away. Nothing fictional can survive its touch. Even the cool blue light of the blue moon recoils from it. Each slashing smudge oozes with the anger you felt as you erased Rulette's story. You wanted to rub every trace of her out of Astorya. And it shows. You don't regret it, but you can't deny the hideousness of the aftermath.

From where you stand, the edge of the GPS looks like a dark horizon against the swirling erasure. The silhouettes of your friends stand out in stark contrast. Heads bowed, they search the ship's surface for Originals.

"Found one!" Ember's voice calls out into the night. Squinting, you can just make out the shape of the tiny ninja.

"Hey-ho!" you hear Prince S. rejoice from somewhere behind you. The other Couriers echo his call from across the surface of the ship.

"Let's go see what she found," you say.

"Ah *oui!*" The stoat perks up.

You take a bold and carefree step forward. Pain as sharp

as the S. Word[5] shoots through your leg from your laser wound.

"Ow!" you cry.

"Zee leg still giving you trouble, eh?" Manteau says. "Zat's what happens when you go charging into danger. You always have to be zee brave one!"

"Would you prefer to still be in the dungeon right now?" you ask.

Avoiding the question, Manteau muses from atop your shoulder, "I hope Ember found zee story of *Zee Little Cheese Dancer*. I could not bear to lose zat one!" Whether that story concerns someone who dances on little cheeses or a little cheese that itself dances, you can't say.

Soft as it might be, the ship's stool surface offers little relief for your injured leg. As you take a few hobbling steps toward Ember with Manteau clinging to your shoulder, you hear a strong voice call out from behind.

"Halt!"

The voice speaks with such command that it almost stops your heart along with your legs. You turn to see the intimidating form of Alicole, half winged horse, half lady sheriff, all Pegasus-centaur.[6] As she gallops toward you, the

---

5 Prince S.'s legendary sword, in case you thought we meant something else
6 Pegataur

blue moonlight shimmers on her majestic golden wings. "I cannot allow you to suffer your battle wounds," she says, reaching down to you. "That would be no way to honor the savior of Astorya."

Before you can reply, she throws you onto her back. Manteau clings to your neck to hang on.

"I have never seen Alicole take to someone like this." The stoat's whiskers tickle your ear as he speaks softly into it. "She must really like you."

A plume of pride swells up inside you. This incredible, mythical, no-nonsense force of nature likes you. You marvel at how far you have come with her. It feels like just yesterday[7] that she broke your pencil in half for erasing your car, and then looked at you like she wanted to break you in half, too. Vanquishing Rulette must have earned her forgiveness, even if you did have to use your eraser to do it. You wish Manteau could get over it as quickly.

Alicole trots forward with you and Manteau bobbing gently on her back. A glint of silver catches your eye. You look in its direction and see Nova. Her silver jumpsuit sparkles as she strides. For someone who should be gangly, being so tall and thin with such long legs and four arms

---

7 That's because it was just yesterday.

of varying lengths, she moves with surprising grace. But you find everything about Nova surprising. She's an alien. She can camouflage herself to the point of invisibility. And she's basically a living supercomputer with a brain so powerful it can reach across space and right into the thoughts of others. She could even be reading your mind right now. *Are you?* you wonder. *Wave if you are.* No sooner do you think the thought than Nova smiles and waves in your direction with her second-longest arm.

"So cool," you murmur, amazed at the powers of the femalien chamalien.

"I know," Manteau replies. "Alicole has never offered me a ride."

Before you can even consider clarifying what you meant to Manteau, a large dark form rushes into view. Startled, you jump. After a second, you realize that it's just Larry, the giant dung beetle. You feel a little embarrassed, getting scared by him like that. You know Larry would never hurt you. He's the most kindhearted and gentle of the Couriers, despite his unparalleled strength. Still, you can't help flinching when an insect the size of a car[8] takes you by surprise. And like a car, he speeds effortlessly over

---

8 A Volkswagen Beetle, to be exact

the ship's surface. Dung beetles know how to move on dung.

You can't say the same for Prince S.

"Almost there!" he calls out from somewhere behind you. You glance over your shoulder just in time to see him stumble over his buckled shoes and flooncy[9] breeches. Funny to think that he's the leader of the Couriers, since he strikes you as the least commanding of the group. When he's not using the S. Word, he seems rather hapless. And not just because of his lack of physical fitness or the ridiculous clothing he wears, but because of his terrible memory. Now, you realize you have memory problems of your own, and you don't fault Prince S. for not being able to remember his last name, but he often fails to remember the most crucial pieces of information as well, like the words to open the starway.[10] You still find Prince S. gracious and charming, but you just wouldn't want to go following him off the ends of the earth.

Up ahead, you see Larry reach the ninja first. Alicole picks up the pace and arrives not far behind. She kneels and you

---

9 If you saw Prince S.'s pants, you would come up with that word, too. It's close to "flouncy," which means an ornamental fabric drawn in with pleats or frills, but with an extra "o" for its extra oomph.

10 The secret star stairway that crosses dimensions and the theoretical best way to get you home. Too bad the next one opens in 338 years.

slide off her back. Manteau leaps off of your shoulder and bounds over to Ember's side.

"Thanks, Alicole," you say.

Nova steps up alongside you, followed by a winded Prince S.

"What story is it?" Larry asks the little ninja in his doughy, dopey voice.

"It's impossible to read," Ember says, studying the story in her hands. Those hands look so small and innocent,

but you know they can magically generate fire and smoke whenever she pleases.

"Back away, everyone," Prince S. commands, "we are blocking her light."

"No," Ember replies, "light won't help." She holds up the crap-caked page. "See?"

"How did you ever find it?" Manteau asks.

"I was close to the ground," Ember says, "not riding around on someone's shoulder."

"I don't know what you're talking about," Manteau says as he climbs back onto your shoulder. Ember watches him. Her judgment smolders beneath her ninja mask. You feel like you should apologize, even though you have no control over where Manteau decides to sit. Physically, Ember isn't much more imposing than Manteau, but she definitely intimidates you the most of all the Couriers.

"I'll take care of that for you," the dung beetle says, and snatches the filthy sheet of paper. He plucks chunk after chunk off the story, dancing as he munches, making the flecks of copper and green on his black shell sparkle like fireworks.

Larry's frolicking defuses the tension. You feel grateful that he smoothed over the brewing trouble between your friends. No one really wants to endure a spat between

Ember and Manteau, however entertaining it might be.[11]

Larry devours the last nasty morsel from the page and holds it aloft. It gleams in the blue moonlight. Everyone claps and you try not to think about what he just ate.

"Behold!" Prince S. cheers, waving his feathered hat. "Another Original redeemed from the false queen's devilry!"

"It's *Galfalador*," Ember says, reading the title.

"*The Onyx Unicorn of Splendidia!*" Larry says excitedly.

"*C'est bon*," Manteau says, "but zee search for *Zee Little Cheese Dancer* continues."

"How many more stories are still missing?" you ask.

"We don't know how many Rulette stole," says Alicole, "nor how many her Rubots erased."

"Nova, can you take a guess?" you ask. You can't imagine Nova, with her big femalien brain, shying away from making a difficult calculation.

"You are correct to observe that I enjoy complex computations," Nova says, reading your thoughts. "Analyzing my memory of the height and width of the story piles in Rulette's dining hall shows the number of Originals left to collect to be approximately twelve thousand eight hundred two."

---

11 Between Ember throwing fireballs and Manteau pulling fire extinguishers out of his coat, it could last until dawn.

While the figure Nova landed on does not give you much hope for rounding up the lost stories anytime soon, the fact that she can make that kind of estimate at all fills you with awe.

"And how many have we found already?" Ember presses.

"Exactly thirteen," Nova says. Her color curdles to a sickly yellow.

"An auspicious[12] beginning," Prince S. says. "At this pace, we shall discover each and every one of . . . every one of . . . of . . . hmmm . . ."

The knit of Prince S.'s brow tightens as his eyes soften. You can imagine a mini Prince S. diving deep into his own mind, searching for the sunken treasure of whatever it was he was saying.

"I told you, it ain't me!" You hear the unmistakable sound of Banjoe the banjo's twangy voice approaching.

"You don't bathe," bellows Baron Terrain. "And the smell is intolerable."

"Boss," Banjoe pleads, "I swear, I don't make smells! Banjos don't even sweat!"

"When are we going to ditch those two?" Ember whispers.

---

12 Promising, encouraging, or even just good. In other words, the opposite of what everyone's feeling right now. People in leadership positions often say the opposite of what they really mean.

"As soon as possible," says Alicole. You can tell she would rather be blasting the two bandits with rainbolts,[13] locking them up in her county jail, or otherwise thwarting their criminal minds than abiding their presence. You, however, don't really mind them tagging along. While you find Banjoe and his songs mildly annoying, he's occasionally entertaining. And Baron Terrain, though extremely full of himself (and there's a lot of himself to fill), proved himself useful in battling the Rubots.

Baron Terrain sidles his mountainous body up to the group with his little musical sidekick close on his spurs.

"I apologize for my hench's stench," the Baron announces. "I know he stinks. Stinks so bad I can taste it."

"You can smell him over the ship?" you ask. Your nose has grown so accustomed to the rank odor wafting up from the surface, you doubt you could smell even Grimy Jim[14] right now.

"The ship?" The Baron's voice drops.

"Yeah," you say. "Haven't you noticed?"

Baron Terrain looks down at the dark matter at his feet. His nose twitches, causing his stiff mustache to spasm.

---

13 The searing electric rainbows that her crossbow fires. You wouldn't want to find yourself at the end of one of those rainbows.
14 Another member of Baron Terrain's gang, the Despicable Six, the one you can smell from a mile away. Luckily, he's many miles away.

"You mean," he quavers, "it's true what they say? This ship is made of . . . of . . ."

"Poop!" Larry says proudly. "Isn't it great?"

Baron Terrain's face freezes in flabbergastation.[15] He gingerly raises and lowers one of his mammoth feet and then the other, then lets out a high-pitched squeal—much higher than you thought a man of his size could produce.

"Get me off it!" he shrieks, flapping his beefy arms as if that might give him the ability to fly. He lobs himself at Alicole in a pathetic attempt to get on the Pegataur's back.

"Don't you dare!" Alicole shouts, rearing up on her powerful back legs. You can't suppress a smile, thinking of how she just gave you a ride.

Baron Terrain looks around like a trapped animal and decides to clamber up onto Larry's

---

15 The state of being flabbergasted (astonished, dumbfounded). Not to be confused with a "flabby ghast station," which would be a meeting house for ghosts made of soft, loose flesh. Why a ghost would have any flesh at all is the real question, let alone why there would be enough flabby ghasts around to need their own meeting house.

shiny carapace. Larry, too nice to protest, grunts under the Baron's weight, but refrains from any other complaint.

"The Originals!" Prince S. declares, coming up for air from the depths of his mind. "That's what I was saying! We must tarry no longer, there are Originals to be rescued!"

"Captain," says Nova. "It is my assessment that the remainder of the Originals are inside the erasure."

"Then all is lost!" Manteau says. "We cannot go in there."

"But we cannot just stand idle," Alicole says. "We are sworn to protect those stories. We must enter."

"Entering would not be advisable," Nova says, her skin shifting to the alarming orange of a traffic cone. "The erasure degrades and eventually destroys all fictional elements within its boundaries."

"Wait one finger-pickin' minute," Banjoe says. "If them stories are in that there mess, how do you know they ain't been destroyed?"

"Because they're from the real world," you say. "Right?"

"By my honor, you speak the bare truth!" says Prince S. "'Tis well known, but worth repeating, that the Couriers valiantly sail upon the Galick Sea to bring back these Original stories from your world so that they may come to life here in Astorya."

"But the actual paper the stories are written on is real," says Larry.

"Obviously," Ember mutters, barely loud enough for you to hear. She seems even sulkier than she did in Rulette's dungeon.

"And due to your success in Spielburg," Nova says, rolling over Ember's eye-rolling, "we know now that nonfictional items can survive the erasure."

"Then I'll have to go in there alone," you say.

"But zat will take forever," Manteau says.

He's got a point. Twelve thousand eight hundred two is kind of a lot of stories. Not to mention your impaired mobility in there. You think back on your arduous journey through the erasure of Spielburg, how the foggy nothingness seeped into your pores and threatened to suffocate you until you realized you had the power to—

"Write!" The word leaps off your tongue. "I can write something to fill in the erasure!"

"*C'est magnifique!*" cheers Manteau. "Get rid of zat awful erasure!"

Green stripes of excitement race over Nova's skin. "By writing a new story to replace the erasure," she says, "we can all enter safely and retrieve the Originals."

"Brilliant plan!" Prince S. declares. "A new setting!"

"Please!" says Baron Terrain, still teetering on Larry's back. "Somewhere sanitary!"

"Yeah," Larry adds, "somewhere with extra poop!"

"What's sanitary about that?!" Baron Terrain yells.

"Everything!" The dung beetle bucks with glee, accidentally knocking the Baron off his shell and onto the GPS. *BOOF!* The bandit lands flat on his back and swings his limbs in a mad attempt to get up, but succeeds only in making a poo angel. He wails in exquisite agony.

Trying to block out the Baron's hysteria, you narrow your mind to the question of what to write. You take out your pencil and remember that you lost your notebook when the Rubots erased High Yah and the mountain vanished beneath your feet. You fell into the Fanta Sea and your notebook sank to the bottom of that purple soda ocean. Too bad, you could really use something to write on right now. But you have another piece of paper, the one that once told the tale of Rulette's tyranny, the one you erased. It seems only fitting that whatever replaces her terrible reign should be written on the same page.

"It should be a mountain o' gold!" Banjoe shouts at you, sensing your hesitation. "With diamond crust!"

"Don't listen to the bandit," says Alicole. "His mind is

riddled with greed. You should create a stronghold. A fortress."

"A new High Yah," Ember says.

"High Yah doesn't belong in zee Margins," says Manteau.

"Why not?" you ask.

"Zee Margins is a place for Doodlings," he says. "Tic-tac-toe and zat kind of thing. You know, zee throwaways."

Manteau's words upset you. It seems like everyone in Astorya brushes off the Doodlings. But you can't just brush them off. You remember how Rulette cruelly told them that they didn't count because they didn't have stories of their own. And yet, despite the abuse, despite their bleak and depressing existence, despite being forced to dwell in the Margins, they helped you. Maybe you can return the favor. Maybe you can write something for them that will make them feel important, like they belong.

"I know!" you say. "I'll write a home for the Doodlings. A castle of their own!"

"A castle?" Manteau scoffs. "Zat sounds like a bit much for zee Doodlings."

"If it weren't for them," you say, "there would be no Astorya right now."

"*Vraiment? Zee Doodlings?*"

"Yeah. I couldn't have gotten past Rulette's attack poodles without them."

Manteau shrinks at the realization of his own prejudice. "Oh. I did not know."

"'Tis high time to give the Doodlings their due!" says Prince S.

"A palace for a palace." Alicole smiles. "That's fair."

"You can make it the biggest doodle ever!" says Larry.

You ready your pencil.

In case you don't remember how your superpower works (you do have amnesia, after all), you, the one reading this book, also get to write in this book. Don't worry, you won't get in trouble. We promise. And if you really want to make the Doodlings feel at home, fill in the margins with your own doodles. You can doodle the nouns and images from your story, or you can draw whatever you want: scribbles, symbols, furniture, musical notes, unflattering caricatures of prominent political figures. The more doodles, the merrier!

(FILL IN THE BLANKS)

Castle Doodling

In the Margins, where Rulette's castle once stood, there is

a(n) _____ castle. It has _____
　　　　　ADJECTIVE　　　　　　　　　　　NUMBER GREATER THAN 100

rooms. Doodlings from all over the Margins come there

because it calls to them like a(n) _____ , it makes
　　　　　　　　　　　　　　　　　　　　NOUN

them feel very _____ , and they each get their
　　　　　　　　　ADJECTIVE

own _____ . There is a(n) _____ dining
　　　　NOUN　　　　　　　　　　　　　　ADJECTIVE

hall in the center with a long table that can fit several

_____ .
　　PLURAL NOUN

"Oooh!" Banjoe hoots. "There should be food! With dippin' sauce!"

"The palace must be able to withstand any attack," says Alicole.

"It needs someplace to train," says Ember, "like a dojo."

"Include a laboratory," says Nova.

"A shower," whimpers Baron Terrain.

"Ample verdure!" says Prince S.

"Huh?" you say.

"You know . . . ," Manteau pipes up, "*végétation*. Foliage. Greenery. Plants?"

Sheesh. Talk about design by committee. You sigh, trying to accommodate all your friends' suggestions.

It has a gym with a(n) _____ where you can

NOUN

practice _____ and a trampoline that you

VERB ENDING IN "ING"

can _____ up and down on. There's a(n)

VERB

_____ laboratory with exploding beakers of

ADJECTIVE

_____ . Many rooms are connected by slides and

PLURAL NOUN

secret _____ . There are all kinds of plants, such

PLURAL NOUN

as fast-growing _____ , _____ trees,

PLURAL NOUN   ADJECTIVE

and flowering vines that smell like _____. There's
NOUN

a pool shaped like a(n) _____ that's filled with
ANIMAL

_____. Every bedroom has its own _____
LIQUID   ADJECTIVE

_____ for _____. The walls
NOUN   VERB ENDING IN "ING"

are made of _____ , so it can _____
NOUN   ADVERB

withstand any attacking _____.
PLURAL NOUN

Banjoe interrupts you by belting out a rather irritating little tune of his own creation. Apparently, his suggestion of adding dipping sauce to the new castle has inspired him. He circles you, hopping and plucking along on his belly as his voice twangs out:

"Wellllll, ain't no cowboy without no hoss,
Ain't no castle without no sauce!
When it comes to dippin', it's the boss,
You know I'm talkin' 'bout dippin' sauce!
When yer dippin' and yer sippin',
And yer fingers ye'll be lickin' and—"

"All right!" you shout. "I'll add the sauce! Just stop!"
Banjoe clamps his mouth shut. You resume:

The banquet hall always has _____ *food*
ADJECTIVE

with lots of dipping sauce, like _____,
DIPPING SAUCE I

_____ *, and* _____ *. Castle Doodling*
DIPPING SAUCE 2   DIPPING SAUCE 3

looks like this:

(DOODLE YOUR DOODLING HOME ABOVE)

You look up from the page and see your awesome new setting before you. It has stamped out every trace of the erasure. Laying your eyes upon it fills you with warmth. Where once a place of horror stood now stands a place of happiness. No longer will the Doodlings feel marginalized with a home like this at the Edge of the World. And they've got a view of the Galick Sea right out the window. No doubt about it, you've created quite an impressive chunk of real estate.

"Bravo!" cheers Manteau, clapping his paws.

"You've authored such a wonder," says Prince S., "it beggars all description."

"A new day dawns for the Doodlings," says Alicole.

Banjoe tugs at your pant leg. "Did you remember to put in the dippin' sauce?" he asks, his teeny eyes full of hope.

"Yeah," you say, "I did."

"Yeehaw!" Banjoe hollers. "Then let's get on over there and eat!"

Oh, right. Eating: that delightful activity that you have to do to stay alive. Your mouth floods in anticipation. With all the adventuring you have done, you have not had nearly enough to eat. You saved Astorya, you deserve a hero's feast.

"A precipitous onset of caloric intake would be highly beneficial," Nova says.

"Aye," Prince S. says. An opening expands on the surface of the ship in front of him. "Be not the last one in or be a rotten quince cake!" He laughs and leaps inside.

"Into zee poop chute, everyone!" Manteau shouts with glee, springing off your shoulder. The little stoat dives headfirst into the hole.

"P-p-poop chute?" Baron Terrain, who has managed to scrape his quivering self up and out of his poo angel, blubbers at the news that his future holds yet more excreta.[16] "No! I can't. I can't do it!"

"Don't make us late, Baron," Alicole snarls. "We have more important things to attend to than you."

Alicole unfurls her wings and with a single stroke, lifts herself up off the ship and then swoops down inside. Ember somersaults through the air and flips into the hole. Nova lopes to the chute and slips in. Larry scampers over and drops himself down.

"Sorry, boss," Banjoe says. "Gotta follow them goody-two-boots!" And before the Baron can even wipe enough of his tears out of his eyes to see, Banjoe takes his spindly

---

16 A fancy way of describing waste matter discharged from the body. Try using it in polite company the next time you have to use the restroom.

little legs across the muck and jumps in.

Baron Terrain looks at you. His eyes, swollen with tears, glisten in the blue moonlight. He hardly seems like the brash criminal you met in Sarsaparilla. He has been undone by dung. You can't help but feel sorry for him. "Don't worry," you say, reaching out your hand to his filth-encrusted glove. "It's really clean inside the ship. Like, eat-off-the-floor clean."

"But, but, what could be in there, but more . . . more . . . p-p-p . . ." His trembling lips cannot bear to form the word.

"Trust me," you say in such a commanding way that you surprise yourself.

It works. The lumbering bandit heaves himself onto his feet and trudges with you over to the hole. You worry what will happen if he freezes and refuses to jump in, as you are nowhere near strong enough to push him. But his will has been broken, and when the opening stretches wide, flooding your nostrils with the strangely sweet air of the chute, he grabs your hand and together you hop in.

CHAPTER TWO

*H*and in hand (since the Baron will not let go), you drop into the chute. A beam of blue light blooms up from below and catches you, easing your fall. As you drift downward, bathed in the fresh air and cool glow, the Baron relaxes his grip on your hand. A moment later, the light places you both on the ground and dissipates, leaving you in darkness.

ZSCHOOM! The door to the main cabin of the GPS opens in front of you.

"Come on in!" Manteau calls out.

"This is going to be a little weird," you caution the Baron as you approach the door. "But just walk through."

Still recovering from his trauma on the surface, he

moans softly but shuffles along after you.

You wade into the blinding light spilling from the doorway and step inside. As your foot finds no floor on the other side, you fall. But, thanks to the gravity inverter of the ship, you land on your feet, as if you hadn't fallen at all, but instead had stepped onto the wall below the door.[17] The ship's interior, distinctly more metallic and less forgiving than the exterior, doesn't feel great on your wounded leg. Wincing, you quickly move aside as you hear the Baron lurch through the door.

After so long in the dim light outside, you must shield your eyes from the bright lights and dazzling cleanliness of the ship's cabin. The Baron lands beside you, dazed from both the sudden change in illumination and the strangeness of the gravity inverter. The door shuts behind him. *ZSCHOOM!*

"Everyone's in!" you hear Larry call out above you. You look up and see your friends smiling down at you.

"What took you so long?" Manteau asks.

"What do you think?" You nod toward the Baron, whose eyes have adjusted to the light and now see the extent of his filthiness.

---

17 As you may recall, the whole concept of walls and floors does not really apply inside the GP3, as you can stand anywhere inside the hollow sphere of the ship and always remain right side up.

"Now you see the truth of yourself, Baron." Alicole's voice bears down over him. "Dirty inside and out."

"Sheriff," he sobs, "please . . . Get it off me . . . I'll never be bad again. Thieves' honor!"

"Don't make promises you can't keep," says Alicole. "Larry, put him out of his misery."

"I'm on it!" the dung beetle says, racing around to the Baron's side. If she had asked Ember to put him out of his misery, you would be worried that Baron Terrain was about to go up in smoke. But you know that the bandit has nothing to fear from Larry. He picks clean the plate that is Baron Terrain.[18]

Free from filth at last, he throws his arms around Larry. "Thank you!" he snivels with tremendous gratitude. "I owe you my life. How can I ever repay you? I'd marry you, but I'm not the marrying type."

"Um . . . Thanks?" Larry says, trying his best not to sound uncomfortable.

"Nova," Prince S. says from the command chair, "take us thither to Castle Doodling."

"Aye, Captain." The chamalien extends her longest arm over to a panel of flickering lights. "We shall arrive in one hundred seventy-six seconds."

---

18 Poo-poo platter

"Let's turn on zee World View," Manteau says.

Nova nods and pulls a lever next to her. In an instant, the gleaming metal and flashing lights, the dungy exterior, every trace of the GPS vanishes. You and your comrades appear to float in midair.

"AAAAGH!" Banjoe screams and flails his rickety limbs. "We're all gonna fall!"

"The ship is still here," says Nova. "It has simply become transparent."

"Don't overreact," the Baron chastises his hench-instrument. "You're embarrassing yourself." A little cleanup and he's back to his old self again.

You don't want to embarrass yourself, either, but the sensation of flying with no ship around you makes you woozy. Whether it's the actual movement of the ship or just the sight of the ground moving below you, you can't keep your balance. You stumble, which causes pain to shoot through your injured leg. You take a long, deep breath, and try to keep your cool. Ember throws you a look. Apparently, not cool enough.

Of course, the ninja can handle whizzing through the air like this. She does it all the time, usually while flipping. She's fictional, so she's never really been injured. Ember darts over to you. You steel yourself for her commentary.

"Do you still miss your home?" she asks.

Her question stuns you.

"Of course," you say. Although it's a little more complicated than that. Since Rulette hijacked your starway and stranded you here, you hadn't really thought too much about home. And that was kind of nice. You felt free from the despair of your amnesia. Now the ninja's question has returned that heavy cloud of not knowing who you are and where you came from and how to get back there to your mind. You wonder if she's deliberately trying to upset you. "Why?" you ask.

"I was just wondering because"—both her gaze and her volume drop—"I've never lost a home before High Yah."

"Oh," you say. Twinges of guilt tug at your heart for assuming the worst of this little ninja. She wasn't trying to hurt your feelings. She's grappling with her own. And while your home continues to be a mystery to you, you're pretty sure it wasn't erased out of existence.

"Prepare for landing," Nova announces as she flips the World View lever back up. The interior of the ship reappears around you. Abruptly but softly, the ship comes to rest on the ground. *BOOMPH!*

Manteau scampers over and climbs up to his perch on your shoulder. "Why are you looking so glum? We are about to take a tour of your latest, greatest creation! *On y va!*"

You force a smile to appease Manteau, but your thoughts hover around the idea of home. Your companions file toward the door and you follow.

ZSCHOOM.

"Do you think I'll ever see my home again?" you ask Manteau.

"*Absolument!*" he replies as the soft blue light of the poop chute engulfs you. "You know zat if you did not make it home, none of us would be here right now. You write zee *Story of Astorya* from your home in zee future and it arrives here in zee past."

"But you said there won't be another starway for over three hundred years. So how do I get home?"

"I have no idea! But we live in an infinite universe, *non?*"

"So . . . there are infinite ways for me to get home?"

"*Non.* Probably not. But one or two, *peut-être.*"

"Like what?"

"Maybe zee next time we sail across zee Galick Sea, we can do a little exchange. Zee stories from your world come in, maybe there is a way for you to go out."

Doesn't sound like much of a plan, but it's enough to give you hope.

The soft blue light deposits you and your party onto the

grayish ground of the Margins one by one. Much to Baron Terrain's relief, you don't have to scale down the filthy surface of the ship.

Looking up, you behold the splendor of Castle Doodling towering over you.

"Whoa!" Larry says, his voice overflowing with wonder. "What a cool castle!"

Alicole gives you a nod. "Outstanding work."

"Thanks," you murmur, finding it hard yourself to believe how well it turned out. You can't wait to see the inside. Sudden fascination with the castle eclipses all your worry about being stranded in this world.

You see movement at the castle entrance. Straining your eyes through the shadowy moonlight, you make out ten skinny figures gathered around the front door.

"The stick men!" you realize aloud. "They're already here!"

"You know these stick people?" Manteau asks, discomfort in his voice.

"Yeah!" you say, limping toward them. "You gotta meet them! I can't wait to see the looks on their faces when I tell them this castle is theirs." The stick men turn to greet you.

Oh, you think. *Right. They don't have faces.*

The stick men enthusiastically pantomime[19] their joy at seeing you again. Sphincter, the first stick man you freed from the Hanging Gardens, tenses up his already rigid stick frame and gives you a stick salute. You grab hold of his stick torso and pull him in for a stick hug. The others layer around you, giving you a stick group hug, but a silent stick group hug (unless you count Manteau, who pants with fear). The rest of the Couriers and the two tagalong bandits join you at the front door of the palace.

Sphincter bows before your friends. All the other stick men follow his lead.

"This is Sphincter," you say. "He's the leader of the stick men. Sphincter, this is Prince S., the captain of the Couriers."

"Well met!" Prince S. says. "What did you say your name was again?"

From the look on his face, you guess that Prince S. doesn't encounter the word "sphincter" too often. Most people don't, unless they enjoy reading medical textbooks. Other people think it's a rude word. But, however you feel about it, everyone has sphincters. You couldn't live without them. Ask any doctor.

---

19 To express something without talking by making exaggerated gestures, like charades (except in the case of the stick men, their game of charades never ends)

You look out at the dreary landscape of the Margins and see movement. Something approaches over the crest of a distant hill. Many somethings.

"The Doodlings!" you say. "They're on their way!"

Your friends gaze out over the featureless countryside. Wave after wave of Doodlings cascade down the hill, bounding closer with an enthusiasm no Astoryan has ever witnessed. Rows upon rows of random scribbles, legions of logos, platoons of polygons, throngs of thingamajigs, and hordes of whosiewhatsits bound toward you. Stars and swirls, squiggles and swooshes, Xs and Os, tics and tacs, smiley faces, frowny faces, neutral faces, hearts, hoops and loop-de-loops, musical notes, and what could only be described as the last scratches of a pen that has just run out of ink—all that inhabits the Margins of this world surges toward you.

"There are too many!" Manteau says, panic in his voice. "They will crush us!"

"It'll be fine, they're harmless," you say, trying to sound as if the very same thought had not just flashed through your mind.

Before you or any of your party can brace for impact, the tidal wave of doodles crashes into everyone. But rather than trampling over all of you, the ocean of Doodlings lifts

each of you up with a joyous cheer. Much to your surprise, you find yourself crowd-surfing on the doodles.

Their pencil and pen markings feel softer than feathers on your skin. And even more ticklish. Wild laughter erupts from deep within you. You squirm with excruciating glee.

"What are they doing to us?" Manteau cackle-sobs as the living river roils beneath him.

"I don't know!" you cry-laugh in response.

Through the tears of forced joy, you see the Couriers and the bandits in a similar state of sidesplitting surrender, riding the flood of Doodlings. Even Alicole, as serious and proud as they come, brays with unbridled laughter. Borne on a tickle tidal wave, you and your deliriously delighted friends cross the threshold and into the entrance hall of Castle Doodling.

You drift past fine doodle artwork chaotically arranged along the walls. Despite the disorderly look of the place, it feels warm and inviting, much the opposite of Rulette's forbidding Fuchsia Plum Palace. Though you do not find it easy to observe much about your castle as you relentlessly guffaw.

At the end of the hallway, the doodles tickle-tote everyone into a massive dining hall and onto a great stage at the back of the room. It takes a couple of minutes for all of you to recover. Wiping the sweat, tears, and snot from your face, you feel tremendously relieved to be free of the Doodlings, but also sort of miss the exhausting euphoria they caused you.

You look out across the dining hall. The Doodlings scamper about like unsupervised children at an amusement park, giggling and babbling away at one another. You smile at their excitement. They don't even seem to notice the banquet table overflowing with all manner of food (and, of course, dipping sauce) in the center of the room. But you do. You salivate in prefeast anticipation.

"Hooooweeee!" Banjoe hollers. "Look at that grub! Let's eat!"

"Nay," Prince S. commands. "Before our revels, we must gather the Originals."

Banjoe strums a dissonant chord on his belly strings and grumbles something that sounds like "Dagnabbit-ratchefratch."

"With respect, Prince," says Baron Terrain, "my colleague and I are bandits, not Couriers. Therefore, it's only fair that—"

"I wouldn't finish that sentence if I were you," Alicole says with an angry swish of her tail.

"Whatever you say, Sheriff," says the Baron. "If you must go look for stories, Banjoe and I will just wait here . . . and sit at the table . . . with the food . . . and promise we won't—"

Alicole lays a hand on her crossbow, cutting short the Baron's promise and saving him the trouble of having to break it.

Doesn't Prince S. ever get hungry? you wonder. *It could take months to find all those Originals. How many did Nova say there were?*

"Approximately twelve thousand eight hundred two," Nova says, reading your mind. You can't keep your thoughts to yourself when she's around.

You groan. "Why did I write so many rooms in this place?"

A trio of familiar doodles hops closer to the stage. You recognize them as the very first Doodlings you met after crossing through the Great Red Line into the Margins—a peace sign, a smiley face, and a scribble.

"Hey," says the peace sign. "You probably don't remember me."

"I remember you," you assure him. Of course you remember him. It's not every day you meet a talking peace sign.

"Really?" he says. "Well, we never thought we'd see you again."

"Yeah!" concurs the sunny-sounding smiley face. "We were sure you were a goner!" She beams at you. "I didn't think you'd even make it to the Fuchsia Plum Palace."

"Where did this place come from?" the scribble asks.

"I wrote it," you say.

The chatter of the dining hall dissolves into silence. All the Doodlings turn to face you. You stare back at them, a little nervous to find yourself the focus of so much attention.

"Did you say you wrote it?" the scribble asks.

"Yes," you say. "I wrote it for all of you."

The crowd murmurs in disbelief.

"So you'd have a place of your own," you continue. "Castle Doodling is your new home!"

The Doodlings cheer with such fervor that it shakes the walls. They crowd closer to the stage.

"*Non, non, non!*" Manteau shrieks. "Stay back! No more tickling!"

"How can we repay you?" the scribble yells over the rabble.

They don't need to repay you. You didn't write the castle because you expected something in return. Although, if you would like to eat anytime soon, maybe they can help.

"We need to find Originals," you tell the scribble. "Stories. Pieces of paper. There should be tons of them all over the castle. Do you think the Doodlings can help us find them?"

"I'll help!" the smiley face chirps in delight.

"Anything for you," says the peace sign.

A flurry of affirmatives froths out of the masses of Doodlings. Everyone seems eager to help.

Nova's skin shifts to a cautious yellow. "Is it prudent to trust the Doodlings with such a task?" she asks.

"Hrmmmmm . . ." Prince S. strokes his beard thoughtfully. "Which task was that?"

"The Originals?" Ember snarks.

"Ah!" Prince S. says. "That task!"

"It is our sworn duty to protect the Originals," says Alicole. "But under the circumstances, we need all the help we can get."

"The Sheriff is right," says Baron Terrain. "No use letting good henchpeople go to waste."

Prince S. turns to you. "Think you that these strange folk are truly game for the challenge?"

"We can trust them," you say. "The stick men would give their right arms to help us."

"If that is your mind, I suppose many hands make light work. Even if most of them lack hands." Prince S. claps his hands as if to end the discussion. "'Tis satisfaction enough for me!"

You nod at Sphincter. In a flash, he leaps onto the stage. Like a conductor standing before the largest orchestra ever assembled, he communicates to the masses with a few sweeps of his arms. The Doodlings immediately set to work. They roll, bounce, and scoot out of the dining hall, fanning out into the numerous rooms of the castle. Sphincter and the stick men march out after them.

"Now," Prince S. says, "let us partake of this sumptuous repast!"

"If that means eatin', I say now yer talkin'!" says Banjoe.

Drawn like flies, you and your friends advance to the lavishly decked-out table. You can hardly believe the amount and variety of food available. It's as if someone ordered everything on the menu from ten different restaurants. Among the lasagnas and kebabs, salads and soups, you see buckets of dipping sauce.[20] But before you can dig in, Manteau raises his glass.

"I'd like to make a French toast," the stoat says to the

---

20 Sweet and sour, ranch, and mushroom gravy (to name a few)

hungry glares of everyone at the table. *"Bon appetit!"*

Without a word, you and your friends come to the same decision: Silverware just slows things down. You all eat with your hands (or paws in Manteau's case [or pretarsi[21] in Larry's case]). Mouthful after mouthful you cram into your gob. Everything tastes better than you ever remember food tasting. You smile at your fellow diners, who seem to enjoy the food as much as you do. No matter how many servings you help yourself to, the plates of food never empty. You rally, but after an initial frenzy, as your stomach distends and threatens to burst, extreme exhaustion drops over your body. You've been going all day and now that you've lowered your guard, you cannot will your fatigue away.

Casting a drowsy eye down the table, you see everyone else start to slump. Eyeballs grow glassy. Words become mumbly, soft, singsongy sighs twisting off the lips of your comrades and into the late-night air.

"Let's go to bed," you hear someone say. Maybe it was you. You can't be sure. In any case, everyone seems to be fully on board with the suggestion.

Pushing through the thick blanket of weariness, you

---

21 Plural of pretarsus, the clawlike endpoint on a dung beetle's arm. Try not to think about whether or not he washed his pretarsi before sitting down to dinner.

rise from the table and murmur a "g'night" to your friends.
Manteau creeps up your arm and drapes himself around
your neck. Yawning, you make your way into the hall
and stumble into the first bedroom you find. Manteau
is already snoring by the time your head hits the pillow.
Guess he'll be spending the night with you. Stoat slumber
party.

Sleep envelops you in its heavy arms.

CHAPTER THREE

*T*he morning light creeps through the curtains and warms your face. Still in denial of the day, you roll over only to find Manteau curled up on the pillow next to you. His eyes flutter open and after a full-body stretch and yawn (you had no idea he had so many sharp little teeth), his face clouds with a very serious expression.

"Just so you know," he says, "I only stayed wiz you because I didn't want you to get scared." His eyes dart around the room and then back to you. "You know, wiz all those Doodlings doodling about."

"Okay," you murmur. "It's fine."

"And zat was not me snoring."

"There was snoring?"

"Non!" The little stoat stands on his hind legs. "There was no snoring! If you heard snoring, you must have dreamt it. Because I do not snore! So do not tell anyone zat I do!"

"Okay, okay," you say, not quite able to make the same leap from asleep to attack mode that Manteau has made. "Just, please, no more shouting. It's too early." Now free of the covers, you realize you slept in all your clothes, even your mismatched shoes.[22]

"What time is it?" he asks. "I hope we did not miss breakfast."

Your stomach shares his hope, which surprises you after your feastival[23] last night. Hunger demands that you make a hasty return to the endless mounds of munchies in the dining hall. You push yourself out of bed and onto your feet. Your laser wound still aches, but the promise of a breakfast buffet helps dull the pain. You shuffle out the

---

22 You may recall that you had to write yourself a fictional shoe when your real one was carried off by the Dust Bunnies to the Land under the Couch. If you didn't recall that, now you do.

23 Both feast and festival, all in one word. How else would you describe eating until you pass out?

door and down the hall. Manteau scrambles up your back as you limp along, resuming his perch on your shoulder.

"Hold on!" he cries in your ear. "Do you know where you are going? We don't want to get lost. There are a lot of sketchy characters about."

"I got it," you say with confidence. Although you don't really know the way, you feel like you can figure it out. You did write this place. Though your words were not nearly as detailed as this castle turned out to be, with its ornate woodwork and flowering vines slinking along the walls, the whole place feels roughly familiar to you, but more like a distant dream than somewhere you navigated just last night. You must have somnambulated[24] your way to your room.

Up ahead, a lightning bolt doodle flashes across the floor.

"Agh!" Manteau screams and grips your shoulder with his claws.

"Oww!" you howl. "Stop! What's wrong? Are you okay?"

"Fine, I'm fine," he says, his grasp still tight.

"Manteau," you say, impatience stewing in your voice, "you've got to get over your Doodling fear."

---

24 A fancy word for sleepwalking, which is the perfect word to use in a fancy place like a castle

"Fear?" he scoffs. "I am not afraid. I am never afraid."

KAPOWW! An explosion blasts open a door beside you.

"AAGHH!" Manteau throws himself against the side of your face. "Zee Doodlings are blowing up zee castle! I knew we couldn't trust them!" He clings to you by the cartilage of your nose and ear, as if your skull were a bomb shelter.

"Calm down," you say, peeking inside the room. Flasks simmer above Bunsen burners. Pipettes and petri dishes clutter up the counters. "It's the lab. And there's no one in here, Manteau."

"So things just blow up in here all by themselves?" he asks.

A wobbling beaker catches your eye. It bubbles over with a smoking, neon-colored liquid. "Yes," you say, hightailing it down the hallway as fast as your injured leg allows.

KAPOWW!

Manteau launches himself against your face again.

"Manteau," you say, "stop."

"Sorry," he mumbles. The stoat peels himself off your face and returns to your shoulder. If he has another freak-out, he might have to lose riding privileges.

"I wrote this place to have secret passages," you say,

growing weary of walking on your injured leg. "There should be one right around here."

You open the next door and step inside a large room full of punching bags, climbing ropes, and all kinds of exercise equipment. Doodlings chase one another to and fro, ricocheting off the walls in what looks like a combination of tag and bumper cars. A frowny face hurls itself into a basketball hoop while a winky-smiley face leers from the sidelines.

Dodging Doodlings, you venture into the room and walk past a giant trampoline. A troupe of musical notes jumps up and down on it, each hitting its own note when it

bounces. When three bounce at once, they make a chord. The notes spring along, filling the gym with music.

"Not bad," Manteau says, perhaps even enjoying the bouncy little melody.

"I think that's it," you say. At the back of the gym, a line of Doodlings gather at a ladder, which leads to a slide. You watch as a pound sign tumbles down the slide and disappears into a small opening in the wall. The passageway looks just big enough for a medium-size doodle,[25] but you should be able to make it through.

"Zat is not zee way we came!" Manteau says.

"It's a shortcut," you say.

You take your place in line behind a pair of hearts. "We love waiting in line," the hearts say in tiny, sugary-sweet voices. The Doodlings file ahead and soon it's your turn to climb the ladder. "We love climbing!" the hearts gush as they hop up the rungs.

You sit down on the slide. "We love riding the slide!" the hearts say.

"Sounds like they love everything," Manteau mutters.

"WE DO!" the hearts squeal in unison. They cozy closer to you, nestling themselves into your armpits. Manteau, attempting to put some distance between himself and the

---

25 Bigger than a checkmark but smaller than a game of tic-tac-toe

Doodlings, climbs on top of your head. You push off down the slide, and the hearts giggle as they cuddle you harder.

"Manteau, watch out," you say as you slide toward the opening in the wall. Manteau may only measure one foot tall, but that's one foot too tall to fit through the portal.

"AAGH!" he cries and dives into your lap, where he finds himself sandwiched between the two adoring Doodlings.

"We love stoats!" they declare as they nuzzle his soft fur. He squirms in supreme discomfort. Ducking, you slide through the passageway and move along horizontally through a dim corridor.

Down, up, sideways, this-ways and that-ways you go. All in all, the experience is more of a roller coaster than a slide. But unlike a roller coaster, with its tedious climbs and lunch-losing plummets, your speed on the slide never changes. You just cruise along at a comfortable clip. No wonder the hearts love it so much.

The slide levels out and carries you past an enormous glass wall. Through the glass, you see the shoreline at the Edge of the World. The glittering black waves of the Galick Sea crash into the coast. Something else catches your eye on the landscape. Closer in, no more than a short jog from the castle, you see a large hole in the ground. It looks perfectly round.

"Look at that." You point out the hole to Manteau. "It looks like it was made by a giant hole-puncher."

"It probably was." He shrugs.

"What's inside it?" you ask.

"*Je ne sais pas*," he says. "I only know zat there are three of them in zee Margins. They call them . . . zee Three Holes."

You remember that Manteau's map had three holes in the margin, but you didn't think much of it at the time. They seemed like the same ordinary holes you would see on any ordinary piece of paper.

The slide bends and the spectacular view of the outside world disappears. You pass through an opening in another wall and slant sharply downward into darkness.

"Wheeee!" the hearts squeal.

Familiar, muffled voices echo about you in the passageway. Another turn, another drop, and the slide comes to an end. Hearts on your sleeves, you roll out onto the floor straight into a sizable pile of paper. *KOOMPH!*

Pushing your head through a ceiling of pages, you see that you've landed on the stage in the dining hall. Mounds upon mounds of paper cover the stage. The Couriers, Sphincter, and Doodlings of all shapes and sizes bustle about the room. The bandits hover by the dining table, snatching scraps of food like vultures picking at a carcass. No one seems to notice you (most likely because you are buried up to your neck).

Manteau weasels his way to the surface.

"See?" you say. "Shortcut."

"More of a longcut if you ask me," Manteau says.

The hearts scamper off the stage. "We love this place!" they cheer.

"Of course you do," Manteau mutters, smoothing out his fur.

You flip through some of the sheets in your paper pile, reading titles like *A Fungus Among Us*; *Mewdini, the Kitten Magician*; and *Hazmata Part 2: Oozin' for a Bruisin'*. "Manteau," you say, "these are Originals!"

"*Incroyable!*" He grabs another sheet and reads, "Zee Mad Scientist and zee Happy Medium!"

"Good morrow!" Prince S. says, striding over to the lip of the stage. "I see you have found the spoils of our dauntless Doodling friends! Sphincter and his sketchfellows have toiled the night through, gathering Originals."

Sphincter salutes you from the floor.

"That's great," you say, wrestling yourself free from the pile.

"I wonder if they found *Zee Little Cheese Dancer*," Manteau muses.

"Now that you have arrived," Prince S. says, "let us break our fast! Hie unto the feasting table!"

Glancing over, you see that in place of last night's dinner, breakfast now awaits you on the table: pitchers of juice, vats of hot cocoa, troughs of oatmeal, pastry pyramids, eggs every way imaginable, heaps of fresh fruit, platters of potatoes, and so many stacks of pancakes, they could stand in for the skyline of a miniature city.[26]

You and the Couriers settle in at the table, where Baron Terrain and Banjoe have already started devouring food in earnest. If the bandits seemed like vultures before, they now resemble vacuum cleaners.

"Don't you two have a town to ransack?" Alicole says.

"I'm thinking about a new occupation," Baron Terrain replies. "Professional eater." He casually pops an entire pineapple in his mouth, spiky leaves and all. People don't usually eat pineapples that way, and from the look on Baron Terrain's face, he's finding out why.

After everyone devours several plates of food, Prince S. surveys the company lazing around the table in a hazy, overfed daze and says, "Now. A matter of great import begs to be discussed." He pauses. "What was it again?"

---

26 As far as dipping sauce, the options now appear to be buckets of maple syrup, hollandaise sauce, and blueberry compote.

"Getting me home?" you ask, hopeful that one of them has a plan.

"Aha!" he says. "That was it! What a pickle . . . what a quandary . . . what a . . . what was I saying? Hmmmm . . . Oh yes! Perchance we may deliver you to your rightful realm by venturing across the Galick Sea into the greater universe beyond."

"But, Captain," Alicole says, "if we intend to leave the limits of Astorya, we must first ensure the safety of the original Original." The Pegataur turns to you. "Understand that while we are committed to returning you safely home, our primary duty is to keep the stories of Astorya safe. Like you, they are real, and so they are vulnerable to all manner of attack."

"Zat is why we keep their locations secret," Manteau says. "Even from each other. So if one of us is forced to reveal our hiding spot because of a Brain Squeezer or what have you, zee other stories will still be safe." His little eyes dart back and forth. "But zat doesn't mean mine are kept *in* a safe! Like zee one behind the portrait of my mother!"

"Otherwise," Alicole says, attempting to cover Manteau's disclosure of where he keeps his stories, "another villain could capture the Originals as Rulette did, and hold them for ransom."

"Say," Banjoe says, strumming his belly, "that's a fine idea, boss. Why ain't we tried that one yet?"

Alicole stomps her hooves with such force that Banjoe breaks a string.

"Should these two really be here for this?" says Ember.

"Yeah," Larry chimes in. "We are starting to discuss secret Courier business now. What if they go blabbing to the Villains Guild?"

"That's preposterous," Baron Terrain says. "We would never do that."

"Yeah!" says Banjoe. "The boss ain't even in the Villains Guild! He never got no invitation."

"It probably got lost in the mail," the Baron mutters.

"The bandits' presence is irrelevant," Nova states. "In order to be effective, whatever plan we devise to protect the original Original must be kept secret from all of us."

"But how can we come up with a plan *and* keep it secret from all of us?" you ask.

"Last time we just let Prince S. hide it," says Larry, "since he has the best chance of forgetting everything he knows."

"Ah, *oui*," says Manteau. "Zee best way to keep a secret is to not remember it."

"So even if another villain like Rulette tries to squeeze his brain again," Ember says, "they won't be able to find it."

"Find what?" Prince S. asks.

"Why don't I just take it with me when I go home?" you ask. You wrote the story, after all; you should be the one to keep it safe. And what could be safer than keeping it far from Astorya and the clutches of the next would-be evildoer?

"The existence of Astorya is predicated on the original Original," Nova says. "If you take it outside the boundaries of Astorya, Astorya will cease to exist."

"Oh." You feel deflated. "But I thought I had to take the original Original back home so I could write it in the future. If I don't have the original story to look at, how can I write it?"

"If you were to memorize the original Original," Nova says, "you could replicate it when you return home in the future, so it can arrive here in the past."

"Memorize it?" you ask. "But what if I mess it up?"

"Don't," Ember says.

Great, you think. *I can't even remember my own name. How am I supposed to remember a crazy story word for word?* You can't believe that the fate of this world hinges on the memory of someone with amnesia.

"So, we have to hide it here," says Larry. "But where?"

"The most inaccessible location possible," says Nova.

"The Land under the Couch?" Larry offers.

"We all know how that worked out before," says Ember, casting a glance at Manteau.

"Zat was an accident!" Manteau protests. "I did not know I was telling Rulette zee hiding spot!"

"Which is why it must be a place unknown to all of us," Alicole says. "But is there such a place? We are the guardians of Astorya. We know every inch of this world."

"Not every inch," Prince S. says. "There is a world elsewhere, a world on the back of this world. The Other Side."

Silence drops on the group like a heavy rug smothering a fire. Everyone becomes still. Even Baron Terrain stops chewing. Everything suddenly feels very ominous. You shift in your seat under the pressure of the room. You can't take it anymore. "The Other Side?" you say.

"Zee Other Side of Astorya," whispers Manteau. "Zat is where zee bad characters go."

"Bad?" you ask, remembering all the fictional things that nearly killed you yesterday. And they were all definitely on this side of Astorya.

"Evil," Alicole says. "Even more evil than Baron Terrain and his gang."

You glance over at the bandits, who don't strike you as particularly evil with their mouths full of doughnuts. *These two aren't all that bad,* you think. *How much worse could the characters on the Other Side be?*

"Exponentially[27] worse," Nova answers your thought. You wish she'd stop doing that.

"You see," Prince S. says, "many yesteryears ago, all characters, good and evil alike, lived together on this side of Astorya."

"The evil characters made it very stressful to live together," Larry says.

"It was impossible to keep the peace," says Alicole.

"Until," says Prince S., "one intrepid adventurer went over the Edge and discovered the Other Side."

"Zat was you," Manteau reminds him.

"Hmmm," says Prince S. "So it was! I thought it sounded familiar!"

"So you banished them?" you ask, trying to keep them on track.

"No," says Larry. "It wasn't like that. They wanted to go."

"They didn't like living with us," says Ember, "any more than we liked living with them."

"They claimed the Other Side as their own," says Prince S. "Now they dwell in that realm of darkness, living out

---

27 A lot. As in evil times evil times evil (that's evil cubed, for the mathematically inclined).

their sunless days in violent delight. And as I discovered, the shadow seeps into the very souls of all who venture there, imbuing them with the evil of the place if they tarry too long."

As Prince S. speaks, you hear the strains of creepy music. It sounds like the kind of tense, spooky tune you might hear in a haunted house movie.

"We don't need the musical accompaniment," says Alicole.

"If you say so, Sheriff," says Banjoe, silencing his strings. "Just thought I'd help set the mood."

"Wait a second," you say, wanting to make sure you understood Prince S.'s flowery language correctly. "If you go there, you eventually turn evil, too?"

"*Exactement*," says Manteau. "Zat is why we avoid it."

"But as fortune saw fit," Prince S. says, "I was able to escape with my good nature intact."

"So the rest of you have never been there?" you ask.

Everyone nods. "Only Prince S.," says Larry.

"But if it's an evil place," you say, "why would the story be safe there? Wouldn't a villain want to go there and take it?"

"If I may speak for villains," the Baron pipes up, carefully dabbing a glob of hollandaise sauce away from his impressive mustache, "just because you are bad, doesn't mean you are stupid. No villain from this side would ever go to the Other Side. You would become so evil that you wouldn't want to return. And then some other villain on this side would take everything you worked so hard to steal."

"Okay," you say. "But what about the villains on the Other Side? If they are so bad, how could you be sure the original Original would be safe there?"

"There is one place down there," says Prince S., "where it would be safe. Where even the most wicked fear to tread. But I dare say no more, lest I reveal too much. That is a secret that must remain locked behind the gate of my mind."

"But what if you forget when we get down there?" you ask. "What do we do then?"

"'We'?" Prince S. says. "You misunderstand. 'We' are not going anywhere. I and I alone must go."

You expect the others to protest, but no one says a word. "But what if you need help?" you ask.

"Did I not conceal the original Original once before and return victorious?" he says with a ferocity that startles you.

"It is logical that the captain go without us," says Nova. "We must not learn the location. If another Courier were to hide it with him, I could read its location in his or her mind. But I cannot read thoughts that are not known to the thinker. Prince S. is the only one who possesses a memory secure even from himself."

"Couldn't I just write something to keep it safe?" you ask. "I could write anything. A fortress."

"Then you would have to write something to keep zee story of zee fortress safe," says Manteau.

"You could write another fortress," says Larry, "to keep the story of the first fortress safe. But wait, then you'd have to write another fortress to protect the story protecting the story. And then . . . Gee, I guess you'd have to write—"

"Infinite fortresses," Ember says.

"Goll durn it!" Banjoe shouts. "There ain't enough room in all of Astorya fer that many fortresses!"

"You have all illustrated the point very well," says Nova. "It would be more efficient to hide the original Original."

"It is decided," Prince S. says.

"I shall journey to the underrealm and secrete the original Original away there. The denizens of the Other Side shall serve as its unwitting guards."

Maybe the other Couriers have full confidence in the abilities of their captain, but you certainly don't. This is the same guy who was taken prisoner by Rulette. He's armed, but what if he forgets to use the S. Word? Or what if he forgets his mission entirely and brings the original Original back with him? Or what if he becomes evil and never returns?

"I'll go with you!" you blurt out to a table of stunned faces. If Prince S. survived the Other Side, you can manage it. Think of all you overcame within the last twenty-four hours.[28]

"*Non!*" Manteau shouts. "You cannot go to zee Other Side! I will not allow it! You are real, remember? You have real consequences! If something happened to you . . ." He shudders. "You cannot be rewritten."

He has a point, and you appreciate him being so protective of you. But you feel a sudden surge of confidence. "Look," you say, "I still have my pencil. I can write my way out of any trouble."

---

28 If you need to refresh your memory, you can always grab a copy of the first book, *Mightier Than the Sword*, now available in paperback.

"Valiant as that may be," Prince S. says, "I must go alone."

"But if I'm with you, I can make sure"—you pause, not knowing how to politely talk about Prince S.'s memory issues in front of him—"you know, if . . . well . . ."

"If both of you go," Nova says, "the chance for success increases by nearly a factor of five." You now feel grateful for her mind reading. She mouths the words "you're welcome" to you.

"Right, because I can be there to help you," you say.

"But Nova could still read your mind and find out where you hid it," Larry says.

"I'll write myself something so she can't," you say. "A helmet of mind-reading-blocking, or something."

"That might stop Nova from reading your mind," Alicole says, "but what if another Rulette comes to Astorya with a Brain Squeezer?"

"It won't matter," you say, "because I'm going back home, right? So I won't be around to have my brain squeezed."

"There won't be any brain to squeeze in zat head of yours if you go to zee Other Side!" Manteau flails in frustration. "What do you think? You can just waltz in there looking like zat? You won't last five minutes!"

You thought the Other Side was supposed to be a den of evil, not some fancy wedding. Who cares what you look like? You snap back at him, "Looking like what?"

"Like a real human!" Manteau bellows with all the power of his tiny lungs. "All of zee scary stories from your world about monsters and nightmares have zee same victim in mind—real human beings!"

"Oh." You hadn't thought of that. "But wait, what about Prince S.?" you ask. Prince S. also looks like a human, albeit a ridiculously dressed one, with his feathered cap, velvet pantaloons, and noisy, big-buckled shoes. If you had to pick out one of you as a target, he'd be it. No question about it. "He's been there. He made it back."

"I have nothing to fear from the likes of them," says Prince S. "I discovered their accursed kingdom and allowed them to people it. They respect me. After their own fashion."

"And what about your leg?" Manteau says. "You can barely walk, let alone run away from zee monstrous horde zat will no doubt want to eat you or do something worse. And you want to go marching in there as a real human?"

Something about what Manteau just said strikes you as funny. Of course you would go marching in as a real human— that's how you go marching everywhere. You can't just make yourself into something else. But wait. Didn't Rulette make herself look like a queen (or at least her idea of one)? Maybe you *can* make yourself look like something else.

"What if I wrote a disguise?" you say. "Like to help me blend in. You know, an evil costume. It'd be like Halloween."

"We're talking about life or death! Not trick or treat!" Manteau shrills.

Prince S. stares at you with eyes that have glimpsed a horrifying world. "What we shall encounter there," he says, "is the stuff of nightmares. Are you truly up to the task?"

You feel your confidence shrink from the intensity of his gaze.

"I think it's a great idea," Ember says. "I wish I could go."

You look at your companions, their faces full of eager anticipation. Deep down, they must know that Prince S. needs your help. Even Manteau, with his quivering whiskers and shiny eyes that plead with you to stay, knows that you must go.

"I'm up for it," you say.

Your friends cheer. Well, everyone but Manteau. He sulks.

"What are you going to go as?" Larry asks.

The dung beetle's question launches a parade of potential monsters in your mind. Vampires, werewolves, ghosts, ghouls, goblins, hags, headless horsemen, banshees, boogeymen, witches, liches, and zombies—

to name a few—all of which would be worthy costume contenders under normal circumstances. But on the Other Side, there are bound to be legions of all those classic monsters. So, if you disguise yourself as one of those monsters, you run a high risk of running into more of your kind. If they don't believe your disguise, they might try to kill you. If they do believe your disguise, they might try to kiss you. You're not sure which would be worse. To avoid all that trouble, you decide to write a monster disguise for a monster that has never existed before. A true original!

You take out your pencil and, finding a space on the back of the page where you wrote *Castle Doodling*, you write:

(FILL IN THE BLANKS)

I have a(n) _____ *disguise that fits me like a(n)*
ADJECTIVE

_____. *It makes me look like the*
ARTICLE OF CLOTHING

_____ *monster anyone's ever seen. Its*
SUPERLATIVE ADJECTIVE

name is _____. *It emerged from the*
PROPER NOUN

_____ *of* _____ _____
NOUN   PLACE NAME   NUMBER

years ago, where it _____ _the inhabitants_

PAST TENSE VERB

with its _____ _____ _and_

ADJECTIVE   BODY PART

_____ _teeth. It's driven by its thirst for_

ADJECTIVE

_____ _and its hunger for_ _____.

NOUN   PLURAL NOUN

It's bigger than a(n) _____, _stronger than a(n)_

NOUN

_____ _of_ _____ , _and_

COLLECTIVE NOUN   PLURAL NOUN

_____ _enough to_ _____ _the_

ADJECTIVE   VERB

_____ _off a(n)_ _____. _Anyone who sees_

NOUN   ANIMAL

_it_ _____ _and feels_ _____ _down their_

VERB ENDING IN "S"   PLURAL NOUN

_____. _My disguise is invincible, so it can't be_

BODY PART

_____. _It looks like this:_

PAST TENSE VERB

(DRAW YOUR DISGUISE BELOW)

I am wearing my _____ *disguise right now.*
ADJECTIVE

Gasps and thuds of chairs falling to the floor wrench your face away from your writing. Your friends leap to their feet and ready themselves for battle—all but Nova, who disappears entirely, camouflaging into her chair in self-defense, and Banjoe, who yelps and dives under the table.

"Not a movement make, creature!" Prince S. unsheathes his weapon. *SCHWING!* "Or you shall know the true meaning of the S. Word."

"We've got you surrounded," Alicole says. In one elegant motion, she swings her crossbow off her back, into her arms, and peers down the scope. "So don't try me."

"I don't know what you did wiz my friend," Manteau shouts, his little voice shaking with emotion, "but I have ways of finding out!" He digs into his magic coat and pulls out a ball of yarn. "*Non!*" He fishes again in his coat and pulls out a lightbulb. "*Non!*" He rummages some more. "Aha! Now tell me what you did wiz my friend. Or face my wrath!" He pulls his paw out of his coat and brandishes a purring kitten, about his size, at you. The kitten pounces on the ball of yarn.

You can't help but laugh at seeing your friends so duped by your disguise.

"Oh, you think zat is funny?" Manteau snaps. "We will

see who is laughing once I begin to dance!"[29]

"It's okay, Manteau," you say, taking off your disguise. "It's me."

Everyone gapes at you.

"It's you!" Manteau's anger melts.

"That's a really good costume," Larry says.

"Your disguise is quite convincing," Nova says, becoming visible again.

"I've never seen anything like it before," the Baron says.

"Master Tanuki said deception is one of the greatest weapons of the ninja," Ember says.

"Thanks," you say, deciding to take what she said as a compliment.

"If that cunning artifice won't protect you on the Other Side," says Prince S., "I know not what will. We shall depart in the space of a fortnight.[30] In that time, your leg can mend and you can commit the text of the original Original to memory. In the meanwhile, the rest of us shall worry ourselves with the collection of the other Originals. Now." He clasps his hands. "I would be most obliged if someone would pass me the maple syrup."

---

29 Manteau is referring to his secret weapon, the Mesmerizing Stoat Dance, which paralyzes anyone who sees it for as long as he keeps it up (in case you forgot that his dance moves are dangerous).

30 Two weeks. The *fort* is short for fourteen, as in fourteen nights, and has nothing to do with how long it takes to build a fort.

CHAPTER FOUR

*T*he time passes faster than you wish. When you're not gorging at the endless buffet table, you spend your days frolicking with the Doodlings (which grows easier as your leg heals) and exploring the bounty of rooms the castle has to offer. You spend your nights listening to Manteau snore (he insists that you are too afraid to sleep alone). And every day, Manteau asks you if you've memorized the original Original yet. Your response is always the same: "Not yet."

During the night hours, you feel the tug of your homesickness the strongest, even though you still don't know where home is. As you lie awake next to the snoring stoat, you wonder what your home is like. You wonder what your friends are like. You wonder if you have a little animal friend of your own back home. Sometimes you get out of bed and gaze out the window at the Galick Sea, thinking of the interstellar voyage that awaits, and you wonder, *Will home be better than Astorya? Will I always feel this way?* Then you get back into bed, take out *A Story of Astorya*, and try to memorize it, but always fall asleep before you even get past the first paragraph.

On day five, a contingent of doodles led by the peace sign rolls up to you. "Look what we found," says the peace sign. A rainbow shuffles over to you and drops a small stack of papers at your feet. Thumbing through them, you see that they are Originals.[31]

"Thanks," you say, not sure why the doodles brought you these, but not wanting to insult their effort all the same.

"Look in the margins," a triangle in the back of their huddle pipes up.

Glancing over the stories, you see several games of hangman on each sheet. It doesn't take you long to recognize their solutions as the ones you solved in the Hanging Gardens.

"Hey!" you exclaim. "It's the stick men!"

---

31 If you're curious, the titles include *Inspector Socks and the Suit Case; Highway 2: The Danger Zone; You, Otter, Know Better: More of Mr. Otter's Biggest Mistakes;* and *Pun Intended Consequences.* To name a few.

Elated to have their Originals, you set about giving your stick friends an upgrade. After borrowing a magnifying glass from the lab, you gather the stick men together in the solarium (the room with the best light). Ten stick figures stand before you, each one in desperate need of some features. Now's your chance to use your superpower to help those who helped you. Give them faces. Eyes, mouths, noses. But don't stop there. Give them clothes. Hats. Shoes. Dresses! Maybe some of them are stick ladies. It's up to you; this is your department.

(DRAW ON YOUR STICK FRIENDS[32])

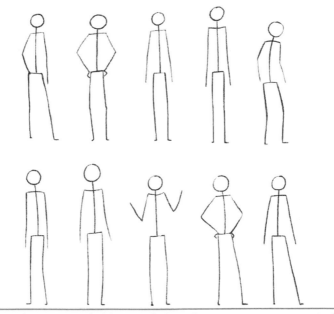

32 Not to scale. We've provided the magnified view here to give you more room to draw.

You finish sketching in the final detail on the last of your stick friends. You didn't think it was possible for them to be happier, but now they are ecstatic. They feast with their new eyes on the wonders your pencil has bestowed upon them. They grab one another and stare, their faces stretching into wide smiles. New smiles. Their first smiles. Tears of pure delight stream down their new faces.

Sphincter grabs you and hugs you. He feels different now than when you hugged him outside the castle a few days back. Before, he felt like a whisper, an outline. Now he feels more complete, more there. And knowing that you've made him so happy makes your heart feel like a rising sun. "Thank you!" His voice rings out like a strong bell. The shock at hearing his own voice for the first time causes him to push you back in surprise. "Was that me?"

"Yes!" you say, laughing.

"I can talk?" Sphincter's new eyes grow wide. "I can talk!" He prances with joy. His voice sounds clean, crisp, full of vigor, heroic even. You can practically hear the Scents of Purpose[33] as he speaks. "Thank you, thank you, thank you, Word Champion!"

---

33 When you shared those scents you got from the Scenter with the stick men back in the Hanging Gardens, you never imagined the effect it would have on them. That's the thing about scents: a little goes a long way. Keep that in mind if you ever apply perfume or cologne.

"Word Champion?" you ask. It almost sounded like he said "world champion." But either way, it's quite a weighty name. It makes you feel like you won some kind of intense weeklong tournament against the greatest brains and sharpest tongues on the planet.

"Yes, you are the Word Champion," Sphincter says. "For you are the champion of our words, those words that held us hostage in the Hanging Gardens. Unless you have another title you would prefer we use?"

"Uh . . ." You stall, sifting through your mind for any glimmer of memory of your actual name. You doubt your parents named you Word Champion.

"Perhaps we should call you Freedom Granter? Or Face Giver? Or Voice Maker? Or a combination to celebrate all of your great gifts?"

"Face Giver Voice Maker Freedom Granter Word Champion!" another stick man chimes in.

"Word Champion's good, I guess," you say, not wanting to end up with Nova's problem of a truly impossible name.[34]

By day eight, your thoughts turn to your journey to the Other Side and you write yourself some gear to aid you in your quest. First of all, matching shoes. You've had enough

---

34 Novagluzsluguzzguzzxzigliguhluhgviggzuh

of hobbling around in one fictional and one real shoe. Next, a vest under your monster disguise to keep your pencil in, so it's always close. You make sure it has plenty of pockets to stash blank pieces of paper, which are in no short supply, for every day the Couriers find erased stories among the Originals and present them to you with heavy hearts. You also write a special waterproof, lined pocket to hold the original Original. Just to be safe, you add that the vest is invincible (just like your monster disguise).

That night, you settle into your bed next to the snoring Manteau and take out the original Original to try to memorize it once again, but your thoughts have other plans. Shouldn't the Couriers have more than one copy of the story? So much rides on this single flimsy piece of paper, a piece of paper that could easily get destroyed by rain or fire or mold or moths or even simple carelessness. If the entire fate of Earth depended on the words written on one sheet of paper, you know those words would be recorded and catalogued one million times over so they could never be lost. Why don't the Couriers do something like that? Surely Nova could figure out a way to store a copy of the original Original.

Or you could just write some kind of device to copy *A Story of Astorya*, which would keep it safe forever. Then you wouldn't have to go traipsing into the many jaws of overly evil monsters. The more you toy with the idea, the more appealing it becomes. You poke the little sleeping stoat next to you.

"Manteau," you say.

"*Non*," he says, still dreaming, "not zee little cheese dancer . . ."

"Manteau! Wake up!"

"Hunh?!" he snorts into consciousness. "What is it?"

"Maybe I don't have to go to the Other Side," you say.

"See?" Manteau says. "It is good I am here, I knew you would get scared."

"No," you say, "I'm not scared. Well, I am scared, but that's not why I woke you up. I have an idea."

"I am listening," he says dreamily, closing his eyes.

"What if I wrote something that could make a copy of the original Original, so that no matter what happens to the paper version of it, *A Story of Astorya* will always be safe?"

"Zat wouldn't solve anything!" Manteau says, his eyes snapping open. "Then we would have to find a place to hide this something you wrote wiz zee copy and zee original Original as well. Zat would make our job twice as hard!"

"No, it wouldn't be like that," you say, realizing the stoat has no concept of how something can exist in a digital form. "I'm talking about making a copy that's not physical. So you wouldn't have to hide it. Then you could make as many copies as you like. And it would always be safe."

"Not physical?" Manteau says. "What do you mean?"

You may not remember your own name or any important details of your life back on Earth, but you haven't forgotten something as basic as a computer. But how to explain it to Manteau? "In my world, we have machines that you can store stuff on."

"No more machines!" he says. "What is wiz you real humans and your obsession wiz machines? We had enough of zat wiz Rulette and her Rubots!"

"I'm not at all like Rulette!" you say, hurt by his comparison. "I'm not talking about Rubots. I'm talking about keeping the Originals safe, not destroying them. I can write something that scans the stories and stores them forever. It's called a digital copy."

Flustered, Manteau throws his tiny paws up into the air. "Our job is to protect zee Originals, not come up wiz an elaborate scheme to shirk our duty!"

"But what about the original Original? I'm supposed to write it from memory in the future. What if I forget something and mess it up? I could ruin everything. If I made a copy, I couldn't mess it up."

"Or you could just memorize it like you're supposed to!" Manteau shouts.

"Forget it." You lie down, but you're too rattled to sleep. Your mind can't help turning over the idea of making a digital backup. If the Couriers weren't so opposed to technology, they wouldn't have gotten into so much trouble with Rulette. They don't even have a way of communicating with each other remotely, instead relying on maps that only show where the other maps are. Not much good if you want to tell someone something. They can't call each other or even send a simple message.

Once you hear Manteau's snoring resume, you creep out of bed and over to the window. If your friends could just see the device themselves, they'd understand what a handy tool it is. Then they'd all want you to write one for them. Who wouldn't want to be more connected? It would be like giving each of them a mobile phone.

Your mind races with possibilities. You'll have to think of every way to prevent the information on the device from being destroyed so that Astorya will never again face the threat of erasure.

After taking your pencil out of your vest pocket and

unfolding a fresh sheet of paper on the windowsill, you write:

(FILL IN THE BLANKS)

The _____ *Device*
ADJECTIVE

I have a device that fits in my _____.
ARTICLE OF CLOTHING

Everyone connected to it can _____ to each other
VERB

and share information _____. It has all sorts
ADVERB

of useful features, like a flashlight, a(n) _____,
NOUN

a compass, a calculator, a(n) _____, and a
NOUN

camera so it can take _____ pictures. It also has
ADJECTIVE

_____ games on it like _____. It can't be
ADJECTIVE · NAME OF GAME

turned off, it never runs out of power, and no one can ever

_____ or delete anything from it, so anything on it
VERB

will always be safe from any _____ *who want to*
                              PLURAL NOUN

_____ *it. It's indestructible, so no matter how much*
        VERB

_____ *it takes, it will never be* _____.
        NOUN   ADJECTIVE

The next morning, at breakfast, you show your friends the amazing device you wrote.

"It looks neat," Larry says. "Good job."

"So, does it shoot lasers or something?" asks Ember. "Like the Rubots?"

"No," you say. Why do they think every piece of technology is an evil robot? "You use it to talk to people and send messages and stuff. But you could also take pictures of the Originals, so they'd be safe forever."

"What if an enemy got hold of it?" asks Alicole.

"It wouldn't matter," you say. "I wrote it so they couldn't erase anything on it. We could even take a picture of the original Original, so Astorya would be safe forever."

"*Non, non, non!*" Manteau shrieks. "Do not do zat!"

"Why?" you say. "What's the harm?"

"We cannot predict the results of such an action," says Nova.

"Forestall your hasty hand," says Prince S. "Tampering with the mechanism of our universe invites chaos and uncertainty to our door."

"Isn't taking it to the Other Side all about chaos and uncertainty?" you ask.

"Zat's zee right kind of uncertainty," says Manteau. "Zat works in our favor."

"Forget it," you say, anger flaring up inside you. "I shouldn't have written it in the first place. I'll just go erase it."

Alicole stamps her hoof on the floor, causing the table to shake and several grapes to roll off it.

"No erasing," she says. "Even though what you wrote is regrettable, we must protect it. Hand over the story of your device."

You know better than to argue with her. The last time you crossed the Pegataur, she broke your pencil in half. You pull the story out of your vest pocket and give it to her.

"Hooooweeee!" Banjoe hoots. "You done made the sheriff mad! Get me some popcorn!"

"How about a slice of quiche?" Baron Terrain asks with his mouth full. "It's delicious."

Frustrated, you bury your device deep in your pocket.

You can't believe they refuse to recognize the brilliance of what you have made. The device would improve their lives, not ruin them. *Maybe they just need a little convincing,* you think.

Over the next couple of days, you corner each of the Couriers to show them more.

"Check this out," you say, handing the device to Larry. "It has a compass. So you wouldn't have to dance with the stars to navigate. It'd be easier and faster."

"Oh, wow! Really?" Larry says. He balances the device between his pretarsi and takes it for a few graceful twirls on the balcony. "Thanks for showing me this, it's really neat," he says warmly, handing your device back to you. You feel the glorious buzz of victory growing inside you. Once Larry gets on board, the rest will follow.

"But," he says, before you offer to write him his own device, "it's a little off. The compass, I mean. It's close, though. Probably as close as a machine can get. But, you know, navigation is more art than science."

With your spirits somewhat dampened, you try again when you run into Alicole.

"It's really useful," you say. "Like if you need a flashlight, you just press here." You touch the screen and a bright light beams out of the device. "See? Isn't that cool?"

"It isn't as bright as one of my rainbolts," she says.

"Yeah," you reply, "but this way you can look at something without having to shoot it."

"I don't have to shoot to illuminate," she says, swinging her crossbow into her arms. She holds a finger over the trigger, and the bolt in the shaft blazes with an electric rainbow light. The little beam from your device can hardly hold a candle to the blinding radiance of her rainbolt.

"Never mind," you mumble as you shuffle away. Her rejection stings, but strengthens your resolve. You refuse to accept defeat. You shall prevail.

Hoping that it might help him with his memory issues, you show Prince S. the device's thesaurus[35] function. But it doesn't help him. He just becomes more and more flustered as he scrolls through word after word, forgetting the word he was searching for in the first place.

Before you even open your mouth to tell Nova about the calculator function, she reads your thoughts and says the screen is not large enough to display the sufficient number of decimal places that she uses in her mental computations.

And when you take a picture of Manteau and show it to

---

35 A book of synonyms, which are words that have the same, identical, similar, matching, or equivalent meanings (we used a thesaurus to write this footnote).

him, he simply shrugs. "So what?" he says. "I already knew I was handsome."

On the day before you leave for the Other Side, Ember surprises you in one of the castle's many lounges.

"You're always looking at that thing," she says, sneaking up behind you as you lie flumped, enraptured by the device.

"Oh, I'm just playing a game," you say, a little embarrassed.

She sits down on the couch next to you. Her perfectly vertical back makes you aware of how bad your posture has grown over the last several days. You sit up.

"Does that help you to not think about home?" she asks.

"I guess," you say, not having really thought about it. You hit pause and offer her the device, hopeful that she might show some interest in it. "Do you want to play?"

"No," she says, "I want to remember. I don't want to forget."

"Forget about getting me home?"

"UGH!" she says, fuming. "All you ever think about is yourself!"

"What?" you ask, blindsided by the ninja's outburst. "What's that supposed to mean?"

"I lost everything!" Ember shouts as a firestorm blows up in her eyes. "My dojo. My ninja friends. Master Tanuki.

And I even brought it up to you in the GPS. And you know what you did? Nothing! You wrote this whole castle for the Doodlings. And faces for the stick men. And even this dumb device of yours. But you never once offered to rewrite High Yah!"

Smoke billows out of her ninja mask. You can only assume it must be pouring out of her ears.

"I-I can rewrite High Yah!" you stammer, dropping your device and reaching for your pencil.

"No!" she shouts. "You can't! Whatever you write won't be the same."

"I rewrote Manteau," you say. "And he's the same."

"You wrote him to begin with! So of course he's the same!"

"How do you know I didn't write the story of High Yah?"

"Do you know what a tatami is?" She narrows her eyes at you.

"No," you say, not daring to bluff.

"Then you didn't write it," she says.

"Maybe I'll find out what it is and then I'll write it. How do you know? I'm the one who wrote you."

"Yeah, you're the one who wrote all of us. And you gave us a mission to protect the Originals. But that's all we have. We don't have a home. We're orphans. None of us belong

anywhere, except inside a giant piece of flying poo. Thanks a lot!" She turns away from you. You think about putting a comforting hand on her shoulder, but you don't dare.

"I was lucky," she says, her voice low. "When the story of High Yah showed up, I finally belonged somewhere. I had a dojo. And a master. And a home. And now it's all gone. And no, you can't rewrite it. You can't fix everything with your pencil."

"Well, what do you want me to do?" She's mad at you for not rewriting High Yah, but she doesn't want you to rewrite High Yah.

"Nothing!" She flounces[36] out of the room in a fury. You watch her go, completely confused.

That night, you lie awake in your bed. Maybe it's Manteau's snoring, or maybe it's the excitement of tomorrow's journey to the Other Side, but you just can't relax and fall asleep. Your thoughts keep orbiting around the little ninja's tirade.

She's a fictional character who lost something fictional. But her feelings are real. The loss she feels is real. Just like the loss you feel for your home. But you don't even remember your home. She remembers what she lost. Does

36 To move in an exaggeratedly angry manner (not to be confused with "flouncy" [see page 18])

that make her feelings more real than yours, even if you're the real one?

Creeping over to the window, you take out the original Original and stare at her description. She's only a few lines on a page. You wouldn't think she would be so complicated. Maybe it's because you are going to write her after already knowing her. Although so far, everything you write here seems more vibrant and complete when it comes to life than the meager words you string together.

You look up at the moon hanging over the Margins. How does this crazy world work?

Why didn't you write her to be happier? Of course she's lonely—who of the Couriers can she really talk to? It seems wrong to you now that you wrote all the Couriers to be so different from each other without giving each of them some kind of home or family or oasis where they belong. The best they can do is hope a story arrives someday that will do that for them, like High Yah for Ember. But what about the others? Do they feel the same? Do they have places they go? Why didn't you write them homes? What if you wrote them in now? Or in the future? Would that be messing with the mechanism of the world, or whatever Prince S. warned you about? Would changing the story destroy Astorya?

It hits you just how much the Couriers are counting on you. Not only to hide the story that you hold in your hands, but to write it. Write it exactly as it is. You wasted so much time in the last two weeks when you should have been memorizing the story like they wanted you to.

Determined not to let them down, you focus your eyes on the page and try again to commit *A Story of Astorya* to memory.

CHAPTER FIVE

"*A*llô?" Manteau's voice speaks right in your ear. You bolt upright and see that you fell asleep next to the window, still clutching the original Original. "Careful wiz zat!" he says. "Zat story makes us all possible. You don't want to get drool on it!"

"Sorry," you say, shaking off the last shreds of sleep.

"At least you've memorized it now, eh?" he asks.

You smile back at him and hope he can't see the failure written all over your face.

"How is zee leg?" he asks.

"Good," you say, relieved to be telling him something true. "Much better."

"*Bon!*" he says. "Today is zee big day!"

After one more all-you-can-eat breakfast, you pack your pencil, a stash of papers, and the original Original into your vest. Before pocketing your device, you thumb through the pictures you managed to take of the Couriers. The images cheer you. You figure that it might be nice to see the faces of your friends when you're stuck on the Other Side, dealing with the worst this world has to offer. You stuff the unappreciated device into your vest, strap on your new, fully fictional shoes, and don your monster disguise—much to the alarm of the Doodlings, who run away from you screaming.

After enough well-wishes to fill a well, a prickly insect hug from Larry, a nearly undetectable nod from Ember, and so many *adieus* from Manteau that you fear you will never depart, you and Prince S. finally leave the castle and head toward the Edge of the World. As you tromp across the featureless ground, a chorus of farewells sings out behind you. You turn and see oodles of doodles crowding every window and balcony of the palace. Having been reassured by Sphincter that you weren't some marauding monster come to claim the castle as your own, the Doodlings now strain to get a glimpse of your departure and bid you a jubilant farewell, cheering and waving—at least the ones who possess the proper appendages to wave. The others just bounce up and down.

Something scampers up your leg, though you barely feel it through your disguise.

"I have decided to accompany you," Manteau says, claiming his perch on your monster shoulder.

"To the Other Side?" you ask.

"*Mais non!*" he says. "I must not know zee hiding place of zee original Original. Zat would spoil zee whole point of you going. But I will go wiz you as far as zee Edge. Just to make sure you don't get scared between here and there."

"Okay." You can't help but crack a smile at his great bravery. With the faithful stoat on your shoulder, you and Prince S. set off again. Your disguise makes walking much more difficult than you anticipated, although your awkward lumbering movements might make you seem more believable to other monsters.

"As good luck would have it," Prince S. says while you push onward, "Rulette fabricated her fortress not far from one of the Four Corners, where I found the waters of the Galick Sea run most shallow. This shall prove our surest hope of passage to the Other Side."

The midmorning sun slides behind a cotton candy cloud, casting a shadow upon the land and doubt into your mind. Your thoughts wander and you grow sweaty in your disguise. You must not be paying attention to where you're walking because Manteau screams in your ear.

"STOP!"

Your foot freezes in midstride. Looking down, you see a gaping hole inches in front of you.

"Zat is one of zee Three Holes!" Manteau says. "And you were about to walk us right into it!"

You take a few nervous steps back from the Hole. Peering into the inky space, you can't tell how deep it goes. Or even if it has depth. Now that you're standing so close to it, it doesn't really look like a hole at all. It looks like a thin blanket of the blackest color you've ever seen stretched out on the ground. A smear of tar, the streak of a permanent marker, even the sky on a starless night seem like mere shades of navy blue compared to the Hole.

"Where does it go?" you ask.

"That is a worthy question," says Prince S.

"Maybe it's a shortcut to the Other Side," you say.

"You and your shortcuts!" Manteau snaps. "Let me see." He slinks down your leg and tiptoes closer to the Hole.

"I've heard murmurs amongst the Doodlings that the Holes are cursed," says Prince S.

"Cursed?!" Manteau yelps and does a backward leap away from the Hole.

"They were afraid of the Hanging Gardens, too," you say. "But that's where I met the stick men."

"You're not thinking of going in there!" Manteau says.

"Why not?" you say.

"Why not?!" Manteau shrieks. "Anything could be down there!"

"All right," you say, trying to soothe the stoat. "I won't go in."

"Good," he says.

"But shall we leave our curiosity so unsatisfied?" Prince S. says. "I think not! Let us investigate further."

Manteau throws up his paws. "You two are hopeless!" he says. "I can already see how it will go wiz you both on zee Other Side."

"Can you find something in your coat we can use?" you say, ignoring his gloomy forecast of your upcoming mission.

Manteau grumbles and begrudgingly reaches into his coat. He pulls out a bright green balloon animal resembling a giraffe.[37]

"I was thinking more like a measuring stick or something," you say.

---

37 Or a dog with a very long neck

"I was getting to it!" Manteau barks. Like a magician pulling a long scarf out of a hat, the stoat reaches into his coat and draws out a large red umbrella. "How's this?"

"That'll work," you say. Maybe not as good as a yardstick or a measuring tape, but at least you can use it to poke around in there. He hands you the umbrella. You creep closer to the Hole and lower the top of the umbrella into it. As the umbrella descends into the darkness, you lose all sight of it. It looks more like an object moving behind a wall than lowering into a hole: Now you see it, now you don't. You probe around with the umbrella but feel no resistance.

"Have you plumbed its fathom?" asks Prince S. You assume he's asking if you felt the bottom of the Hole.

"I don't feel anything," you say, pulling the umbrella out of the Hole. "Maybe we need a longer—"

What you see cuts your words short. Or rather, what you don't see. Without any warning, not a sizzle or a snap, the top half of the umbrella that you lowered into the Hole has completely disappeared. Vanished altogether.

"*Sacrebleu*," Manteau whispers.

"Dear Heavens!" gasps Prince S. "It's gone!"

You lift your halved umbrella up to your face to get a closer look. With nothing to hold it in place, the rest of the umbrella falls away from the handle and hangs around your arm like an enormous red waterproof bracelet with spokes. The missing part of the umbrella doesn't look like an erasure, where a smudgy mess would remain as a reminder that something used to occupy that space. It doesn't look like it got broken off or burned away. It looks more like that part of the umbrella never existed. As if it were made that way (which would make it extremely useless in a thunderstorm).

"Zee Doodlings were right!" Manteau says. "These holes are cursed!"

"But how did it do that?" you ask, stunned. "Where did it go?"

"In truth," Prince S. says, backing away, "this hole has swallowed my curiosity along with the top of that umbrella."

You feel the exact opposite. Your mind grows ever more curious as it tries to make sense of what you just witnessed, but the stoat and the captain want to move on. You offer the umbrella carnage back to Manteau.

"I always lose my umbrellas," he says, tossing the romnants into the Hole. "But never like this." Without a splash or any sound at all, the remains of the umbrella pass into the mysterious void and out of your sight.

"Let us away to the Upper Left Corner," Prince S. says. Manteau scurries back up to your monster shoulder. You all skirt the Hole and continue on your way. But your thoughts keep reaching back.

"Prince S.," you say, "do you think the rest of the umbrella made it to the Other Side?"

"The only way I know to reach the Other Side lies before, not behind us," he says. "And it is not an easy passage. At least it wasn't when I last ventured there. Perchance it will be even more treacherous now."

His words don't offer you much in the way of comfort or reassurance as you lug yourself forward. Your disguise seems to grow heavier with every step. You would much rather be sipping a mug of endless cocoa right about now. Even if you had to listen to Banjoe sing a song about it.

"Look!" Manteau cries, pointing ahead of you. "There it is!"

Your eyes scan the horizon. The dull land you stand on drops off sharply in the distance, both along your left side as well as up ahead of you. As if someone carefully cut the landscape with a giant pair of scissors.

"Tallyho!" Prince S. shouts. He hastens his pace, his

buckles clanking rapidly. You do your best to follow him. After a few minutes of galumphing[38] after him, you find yourself winded, standing at the Edge of the World. Or, more accurately, at the Edges of the World. From where you stand, the two Edges meet at a perfect right angle, forming a corner. It points like an arrow out over the Galick Sea, crashing below and into the vast universe beyond.

Somewhere out there is home, you think. The thought arrests you for a moment. Home seems so far to you right now. But you need to believe that you will get back there. First, however, you must escort this forgetful captain into the heart of evil so you can keep this amazing, weird world you created safe.

"So how do we get to the Other Side?" you ask, feeling ready for the adventure.

"We jump," Prince S. says.

"Jump?!" both you and Manteau blurt out at once. You had forgotten he was on your shoulder. Manteau slips down your monster body. Keeping himself low on all fours, he peers over the Edge.

"AHHHH!" Manteau screams as he flings his body back

---

38 To move with considerable effort in a clumsy manner, just like how it sounds

to safety. "There must be another way. Zat is a long way down. Too long!"

"I'm afraid not," Prince S. says, looking grim. "We must pierce the Galick Sea to get to the Other Side. A great fall goes a long way in achieving that aim."

Steeling yourself, you shuffle closer to the Edge and look down. You can see why Manteau reacted as he did. The Galick Sea roils quite a distance below you. The starry waves crash into the cliff face, bubbling over into surges of foam and stardust.

Vertigo[39] swoops in, making you woozy. *It's okay*, you tell yourself, and try to focus on the glittering waves, rather than the distance between you and them. You match your breath to their rhythm: *in... out... in... out...*

As you stare into the sea below, you notice something strange. Beneath the churning, dark waters of the Galick Sea, you see shapes. You strain your eyes like a person taking some kind of interstellar vision test and realize that they resemble—"Letters," you say. The shapes beneath the waves are letters. And they must be pretty sizable if you can see them from this height.

"Aye," says Prince S. "Letters beget words, words beget

---

39 A sensation of whirling or loss of balance. That dizzy feeling you get when you look over a cliff, window-wash a skyscraper, or have a bad inner ear infection.

sentences, sentences beget stories. Here, where the Galick Sea battles against the Corner, we behold the fraying and mending of our world. Like the corner of one's mind, where thoughts swept away by our busy lives collect and form their own warring kingdoms, the letters torn from the land tussle and toss in the waves below, creating words anew."

His words wash over you like the waves lapping at the cliff below. But you think you understand. Letters make words, words make sentences, sentences make stories, and stories make Astorya. Here, you can see the building blocks of this world: letters swirling in a dark and sparkly alphabet soup.

"I had a theory that Astorya was flat," Prince S. says. "Flat as a piece of parchment. Most thought I was a fool and insisted the world was round. So one day, I set out to prove them wrong. I journeyed to each Corner of Astorya, seeking a spot shallow enough to swim through the Galick Sea and come out on the Other Side. Only when I arrived here and stared down upon the sea, searching for a sign, perchance some divine inspiration, did I find one staring back at me from within the Galick Sea itself. The answer is right there before us. Do you see it?"

You stare down at the waves, puzzled by his words and

equally puzzled by what Prince S. manages to capture in the sieve of his memory. Only a couple of weeks ago, he didn't remember that he discovered the Other Side. Now he seems ready to write his memoirs about it. Maybe returning to this spot has jogged his memory. You can only hope it continues to improve.

"No?" you say.

"*Un moment*," Manteau says. "Are you saying zat there is a secret message in zee waves down there?"

"Yes," says Prince S. "Those letters spell out words below. Words that betray the exact spot to leap into the Galick Sea so that one might pierce its veil. I composed a rhyme so I wouldn't forget it."

"How does it go?" you ask.

"Hmmmmmm." His eyes cloud over. Looks like his memory hasn't improved that much. "Let's see . . ."

While Prince S. scours his mind for his mnemonic[40] about where to plunge into the sea below, you sigh. Once again, you find yourself relying on his questionable powers of recollection. What if he can't come up with it? Does he expect you to just jump in and hope for the best? You

---

40 A very impressive word to know, especially as it has the *m* and *n* right next to each other. It means using a pattern of letters, words, or ideas to help you remember something. Here's one to help you remember how to spell it: My Neighbor Eats Mice On Neapolitan Ice Cream.

didn't come all this way to drown in some cosmic word jumble.

"Ah!" he says at last. "I've got it. It goes:

"*Just beneath the watery eyes,*
Above the sea, the pathway lies.
Follow these words and enter through,
Oh is the doorway right before you."

"Zat is supposed to help?" Manteau says.

You rack your mind to decipher some kind of meaning in Prince S.'s unhelpful poem. Despite the captain's claim, it doesn't seem to offer any clue as to how you're supposed to proceed.

"See?" Prince S. says, pointing to the sea below.

"See what?" you say.

"Beneath the *Is*," he says.

"Everything we are looking at is beneath our eyes," Manteau says.

"Not your eyes," Prince S. says. "The *Is*. The watery *Is* below us."

You and Manteau gaze into the waves, searching for a pair of watery eyes, but you see only letters.

"Do you see the C?" Prince S. asks.

"Of course we see zee sea!" Manteau shouts.

"Excellent!" he says. "Now you can find the path. 'Follow these words and enter through.' O is the doorway to the Other Side. Let us waste no more time!" He readies himself to leap off the cliff.

"Wait!" you shout. "I still don't know what I'm supposed to do!"

"The *Is*," Prince S. sighs. "Once you see the *Is*, you'll see the *C*, and then you'll see it."

"What are you talking about?!" you yell. "How can I not see the sea?! It's all there is down there!"

"Not the sea," he says. "The *C*."

This back-and-forth could go on all day, but we don't want to cause you any more frustration than absolutely necessary. So, in the interest of time, we'll skip ahead to the part where you realize he's saying *Is* and *C*, not eyes and sea.

You look down again at the letters beneath the whirling waves. After a brief search, you find a pair of capital *Is*. Below them lies a letter *F*, nestled on top of a capital *C*.

Now Prince S.'s rhyme begins to make sense. You thought he was saying words when he was actually saying letters. His riddle might help you find the way to the Other Side after all.

"Just beneath the watery Is,

Above the C, the pathway lies.

Follow these words and enter through,

O is the doorway right before U."

(USE PRINCE S.'S CLUES TO FIND
THE WAY THROUGH)

"There!" you say in triumph. "I see it!"

"Where?!" Manteau says, peering over the cliff. "Show me!"

After a few agonizing minutes of trying to describe the location of the phrase to Manteau, he finally says, "Ah. But of course. It's obvious." It's almost as obvious as the fact that Manteau doesn't see it but feels too proud to admit as much. "Good thing I was here," he adds.

"Now." Prince S. turns his gaze on you. "Have you fixed your courage to the sticking place?"

"I think so," you say. "But I don't know if I'll be able to swim in this monster costume."

"That shall prove an asset," he says. "For we seek to sink down to the bottom with a quickness."

"Sink?" you say. "To the bottom of the sea?" You remember when you plummeted into the Fanta Sea and almost drowned in its purple carbonated waters. Now Prince S. wants you to sink in order not to drown? You can hardly fathom it. Your only hope is that Prince S. managed it somehow. "But won't we drown?"

"Fear not," he says. "The bottom of this sea is the surface of the very same sea on the Other Side. And if you stay the course, the sea shall not take you. At least, it was shallow enough to make the plunge in one breath many,

many decades ago, when I last dropped my bodily self into the Galick Sea."

"But it might not be now?" you ask. You don't know about how things work in Astorya, but you know that the ocean changes a lot on Earth. Even minute by minute with the tides.

"Certainty is never within our grasp," the captain replies. "But we must tarry no more. The sun sits on its noonday zenith. Once on the Other Side, we shall have precious little time before . . . before . . . what was I saying?"

Uh-oh. It sounded like he was about to impart a useful piece of information.

"Before what?" you ask.

"What?" he says.

"Precious little time before what?!" Manteau yells. "On zee Other Side?"

"It's no use," Prince S. says. "I don't have time to remember. No doubt it will come to me again. Now." He turns to you. "Capture your breath and don't let it loose till we break through to the Other Side, or it will be your last."

"Be careful," Manteau says softly to you. Not exactly the kind of thing one says to someone about to hurl themselves off a cliff wearing a hulking monster costume hoping to sink.

"Good Manteau," Prince S. says, "if fate sees fit to deliver us home, we shall meet again."

The stoat races up your leg and onto your shoulder. His dewy black eyes burrow into yours.

"I'll be back," you say.

"*Bonne chance*," he whispers and gives your face a hug. Without another word, he climbs down. You inch closer to the cliff and peer over the edge. Your heart batters the inside of your chest like a horse kicking its way out of a stall.

"Remember to aim for the O of *THROUGH*." Prince S. smiles in anticipation of the adventure ahead. "Ready?"

"Yes." Your pounding heart barely allows you to get the word out.

"Onward and downward!" Prince S. hollers and vaults himself off the cliff.

You pull in one more lungful of air and charge after him over the Edge.

CHAPTER SIX

Wind whooshes around your body as you fall toward the dark waves below. You feel like you left your thumping, hammering heart at the top of the cliff. The beauty of the sea strikes you: the glimmer of stardust, the shimmer of the breaking waves, the way it all stays dark yet sparkles in the Astoryan sun. Then the sea itself strikes you.

KAPLASH![41]

---

41 Part KAPOW, part SPLASH

Stunned from the full-body slap, you plunge into the darkness. A rush of bubbles ripples through your costume as your downward momentum slows. Within a moment, awareness floods your senses. Every bit of your being wants to swim upward to the world you know, rather than move yourself farther from the air you need to breathe. But you tell yourself that somehow there's another surface below you.

Cracking your eyes open, you expect to feel the sting of salt water. But whatever fills the Galick Sea feels more like air on your eyeballs, although it hangs heavily on your body like sand. This must be stardust—light and heavy all at once. You're tempted to taste it, but afraid to break the seal of your lips.

A large letter *I* floating nearby glows brightly. Windmilling your bulky monster arms around, you reposition yourself head down just in time to catch the light from the giant letter glinting off the buckles on Prince S.'s shoes. He kicks his way deeper into the darkness, much more adept at navigating the waves in his jacket and breeches than you in your awkward disguise. Regretting your choice of apparel, you do your best to monster-paddle after him.

Every stroke takes its toll. Your muscles quickly grow

weary with the effort. Who knew holding your breath while swimming through stardust in a monster costume would be so hard? Panic seeps into you as the need to breathe takes hold. *Just a little farther,* you tell yourself. Your lungs feel like they may burst. A trickle of air escapes from your lips in a cascade of sparkling bubbles and somehow it becomes easier to sink. Your breath has been buoying you up. *Breathe out!* Though it goes against every instinct in your body, you force the air out of your lungs.

Deeper you dive, down, down, down toward the O of *THROUGH.* Your lungs ache for air. *Push.* Prince S. has disappeared from your sight. No glinting buckles to guide your way. *Did he already make it to the Other Side?* You pump your legs and arms. *Keep going,* you tell yourself. The round sides of the letter rise around you like illuminated stone walls as you descend.

Ahead, you see a glimmering white light dancing through the waves. Another letter? No, somehow, the light looks different, as if it is coming from below the sea rather than inside it. You kick. The light draws you nearer. It feels like gravity has reversed itself. Instead of diving, you seem to be surfacing. You fear the starry waters have

discombobulated you to the point that you can't
tell up from down. But it's too late to reverse
course; you don't have enough air left in your lungs.
Almost there. In a last burst of energy, you push through
the surface and take in a greedy gulp of air.

Something about the air is very wrong. You flail about,
barely managing to keep your head above the waves,
afraid to take another breath.

"Breathe," Prince S.'s voice says calmly. He bobs up and
down next to you, doing his best to help lift you up while
treading the starry water himself.

"I can't." You eke out the words. A wisp of white smoke

drifts from your lips as you speak, like steamy breath on a frigid night.

"You must," he says.

Despite how you feel about the air quality, your need for oxygen wins in the end. You inhale. The murky air worms its filthy fingers into your chest. Your lungs feel like someone set a campfire inside them.

"Smoke!" The word falls off your lips as a fit of coughing overtakes you.

"The air of the Other Side," Prince S. utters. "I cannot say it is harmless, but it will not kill you. Whilst here, we must drink deep of its bitter cup."

You cough until you can't anymore. Your eyes water as your body demands air. You take a quick breath in and swallow it down into your lungs. It still burns, but not as harshly. When you exhale, another white plume escapes your lips and evaporates into the murky air.

"The last gasp from our sunlit side has left you," says Prince S. "Now we shall commence our quest in earnest."

Prince S. splashes off. Light-headed, you paddle after him and fight your way onto a bleak shore. He takes your monstrous hand and pulls you out of the starry waters and onto the beach. You both trudge onto the black sand away from the lapping waves. Though the waters of the Galick

Sea left you dry, the strain of your brief but difficult swim through the stardust weighs on your limbs like wet clothes. That and breathing the thick, foul air exhausts you. But you drag yourself onward.

A full moon hangs high in the sky above, white as bone. It casts a brittle and eerie light on the shore.

"It's night already?" you say. "How long did it take us to get through?"

"Time runs out of joint here," says Prince S. "On the Other Side, it is perpetual midnight, always the witching hour, with ever a full moon."

The constant full moon reminds you of Sarsaparilla, the town where a high noon sun always hangs in the sky, but a creepy, sinister version of the place. You shiver thinking of what other evil mirror images of Astorya await you here.

"Has a chill taken hold of you?" Prince S. turns to you, his face full of concern. Something strikes you as different about him, but it takes you a moment to place it. In the corner of his eyes, where crust sometimes gathers after a long, deep sleep, Prince S. has schmutz.[42] Only rather than the usual yellow or green variety of goop, what has parked itself in his eyes looks red and bright.

---

42 A Yiddish word for dirt or grime or a similar substance you wouldn't want in your eyes

"Are you all right?" you ask, worrying that your dive through the Galick Sea may have injured him somehow. You wonder if he could be crying blood, but you don't want to alarm him. "You have . . . something in your eyes."

"As red as the blood from a freshly pricked finger?" he asks.

"Yeah," you say, disturbed by the specificity of his question.

"Then it has already begun." He sighs and peers into your eyes. "Aye, I see the foulness seeding itself in yours as well."

"Ugh!" you say, not liking the thought of anything seeding itself in your eyes, especially not something called "the foulness." You try to rub it out of your eyes with your cumbersome monster hands. "What is it?" you ask.

"Evil," he says. "Oh! Now I remember! We shall have precious little time before the evil of the Other Side infects us beyond the point of no return."

"How little time?" you ask.

"Likely, fewer hours than fingers on one hand," Prince S. replies.

Now he tells you. You've got less than five hours. And that's only if you believe Prince S. counts the thumb as a finger. He could be a purist who sees the opposable thumb as distinct from the other four, in which case you will have less than four hours to hide the original Original and return.

He resumes walking up the beach. You keep close on his heels. "Evil is in the very air we are forced to breathe here. Mark its progress in mine eyes and know it is in thine as well. We must leave this wretched land before it enshrouds our eyes entirely."

"So our eyes are going to fill up with this red stuff?" you ask.

"Indeed. And it may be that my previous sojourns to this cursed realm have left my hourglass scanty of sand."

"You mean it's going to happen to you sooner than me?"

"That is a distinct possibility."

"What happens when our eyes turn red?" you ask, though you really don't want to know the answer.

"We succumb. We become like everything else in this wayward land. We will see with red eyes and speak with red voices. So watch with vigilance your ideas as they hatch in the nest of your mind, for you will find as the foulness envelops you, your virtuous thoughts will wither and the worst within you will arise, pushing aside your good nature so that your evil nature may flourish. The voice of your mind will redden like your eyes until all your thoughts be red."

Red thoughts? you think. You never thought of thoughts

having a color. You hope you will recognize it when it happens. If it actually does happen to you. A glimmer of hope sparks in your mind that perhaps because you are real, your thoughts will be spared the reddening. But most likely Prince S. is right. You breathe fictional air. You eat fictional food. You jump off fictional cliffs. Just like everything else fictional, the Other Side will likely have a very real effect on you. And even if it doesn't, it will turn Prince S. evil. And you don't particularly want to find out what evil Prince S. is like.

"And there's nothing we can do to stop it?" you ask.

"Nothing," he says. "Except, when you hear the red voice in your ear, hold fast to your fondest memories. They will prove to be the very beacon of your goodness."

My fondest memories. You wish you could summon up your fondest—or indeed any—memories of your home, your family, or your friends. But in your current amnesiac situation, you'll have to concentrate on your fictional friends. That's all right, you've grown quite fond of a certain stoat with a thick French accent.

"So we *really* need to get out of here as soon as we can," you say. "Where can we hide the original Original? Can you tell me your secret now?"

"Secret?" he says.

"Yeah. Where we're supposed to hide the story? You said there was a place down here where we could hide it? Where the monsters are afraid to go?"

"Did I? Well, no doubt it will come to me."

You sigh, already regretting accompanying him on this mission.

"Strange," says Prince S. "I don't remember there being a wall here."

Not a big surprise, considering how little he does remember. Regardless of whether Prince S. remembers it, a wall of sheer rock stands before you. It stretches up to the night sky, a craggy, jutting mass of cruel angles and sharp edges. At its peak, you think you notice something. Either the moonlight fools your eyes, or the wall stirs.

A blast of earsplitting noise erupts from above you and reverberates down the wall. The sound stabs into your ears like icicles drilling into your brain.

"AHHH!" you scream, trying to muffle the noise with your fumbling monster hands. "What is that?!"

"Gnargoyles!" Prince S. shouts. "They must have seen us!"

The wall comes alive with the creatures. Like hornets launching out from a kicked nest, the Gnargoyles leap from their perches and stream into the sky, slicing circles across the full moon.

"Ready your pencil!" Prince S. shouts. "Gnargoyles are made of stone and are just as unyielding." He unsheathes his weapon. *SCHWING!* Delving into your vest with your awkward monster hand, you fumble around for your pencil.

THOOMP.

Within seconds, several Gnargoyles land on the sand mere feet from you.

THWUMP.

Others land and close in behind you. More than three times your size, the Gnargoyles surround you. Their grinning mouths, bristling with horribly sharp teeth, glisten as they snarl, snap, growl—in a word, gnar—at you. Their eyes burn red, full of the foulness of the Other Side. They look much fiercer than the kind of gargoyle you might encounter while scaling the spires of your local Gothic cathedral. Also, they're moving around on their own, which most gargoyles attached to buildings rarely do, if ever.

"Prince S.!" the creatures rasp. Their voices—if you can call them that—sound like gravestones rubbing against each other. The sound makes you wince. You hope they can't see you wincing under your disguise.

One of them lurches closer to you and nods. "O fearsome

one," it speaks, "you have captured Prince S. and brought him here from the Sunny Side. I am sure you know the law—"

"The law! The law!" harsh Gnargoyle voices chant from all sides. You find it rather bizarre that a bunch of monsters would be such cheerleaders for the law. Villains by trade usually don't fall into the "law-abiding" category. They must be heralding a pretty corrupt law.

"Only the fiercest, foulest, most wicked and wretched

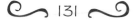

of us all could cross to the Sunny Side and bring back the captain," it continues. "What say you now?"

The Gnargoyles stare at you with their stony red eyes. At least you know they believe your disguise. Not only that, they think you captured Prince S. That'll buy you some time, but you still need to write yourself a way out of this.

You surreptitiously grope for your pencil while doing your best rendition of what you think a creature from the Other Side would sound like. "Uuuurrrrrrrgghhh . . . ," you moan, producing a sound like a grizzly bear with a stomachache. The Gnargoyles look at one another in confusion. Prince S. looks at you, also in confusion.

"Fiendish Gnargoyles," Prince S. says, "I am captain of the Couriers, and I command you all to make way! Else you shall know the S. Word."

Try as you might, your terrible monster fingers can't feel your pencil inside your vest beneath your costume.

"Take his weapon!" croaks one of the Gnargoyles. Its vile voice scrapes against your eardrums.

"Mutinous rogues!" Prince S. flashes his S. Word. The ring of Gnargoyles tightens around you both. Underneath your disguise, you bloom with sweat. "I shall make . . . ," he says, "uh . . . you know . . . those little rocks? No . . . uh . . . pebbles? Blast! Where do my words go?"

As Prince S. searches his mind for the end of his sentence, you search your mind for some way out of this with both of you in one piece. If you help defend Prince S. from these Gnargoyles, they might realize you're not a monster at all and attack you. If you stand back and leave Prince S. to fight his way out of this Gnargoyle knot, they will likely overpower him with their numbers, even if he does use the S. Word. Moreover, they will likely take him away from you. You ask yourself, what would a monster do? And not just any monster. They think you captured Prince S., and as they said, that makes you the fiercest, foulest, most wicked and wretched monster of all.

"Gravel!" Prince S. declares triumphantly. "I shall make gravel of you all!"

"Wait!" you shout. The Gnargoyles turn to you. It's not easy to read the expression on their horrid faces, but you guess they're more than a little stunned by the sound of your human voice. "Prince S. is mine!" you growl as best you can. "The S. Word belongs to me!"

"What?!" Prince S. snaps.

"You're my prisoner," you say. "Remember?" You turn to the Gnargoyles. "His memory is so bad, he can't even remember I captured him."

A wave of cruel laughter erupts from the Gnargoyles and

bombards you on all sides. With them distracted, you try to clue Prince S. in, nodding your head slowly. You watch as the confusion melts from his face.

"Oh!" Prince S. says, catching on. "That's right. I am this monster's prisoner. Now, begone, foul creatures! Let us pass!"

"Hand over the S. Word to your captor!" hisses one of the Gnargoyles.

"Very well." Prince S. sighs. He shoves the S. Word back into its sheath. Unclasping it from his belt, he extends the sword toward you, scabbard and all. You can tell it pains him greatly to do so. The glittering hilt shimmers in the full moonlight. "A word of warning," he says. "Listen to the S. Word. Don't use it."

Not sure what to make of Prince S.'s warning, you take the S. Word from him. The Gnargoyles cheer. At least that's what you think they're doing—it sounds more like a car accident.

A thought erupts inside you: *It's mine now!* You grip the sword's gleaming scabbard tighter. *I don't need Prince S. I could use the S. Word myself. I could destroy these monsters. I could*—you shake your head and that violent train of thought cuts out like it had been sliced off by the S. Word itself. *Was that my red voice?* you wonder. Prince

S. warned you this would happen, but that doesn't make experiencing it any less disturbing.

You awkwardly fasten the scabbard across your monstrous waist with your non-dexterous monster hand. It seems to take forever, but that doesn't bother the cheering Gnargoyle contingent. "Okay," you say, trying not to sound too rattled by their sustained shrieking. "We have to be going now."

"Of course!" yaps one of the Gnargoyles. "To the Colosseum!"

"What?" you say, momentarily forgetting to growl the word in a scary monster voice. You hope they don't notice.

"Surely you know the law," says the Gnargoyle.

"The law! The law! The law!" the Gnargoyles chant, tightening around you and Prince S. like a noose.

"Enough! Enough!" a Gnargoyle's voice rises above the chanting horde. "We must present you and your quarry[43] to the citizens of Monstropolis. Gnargoyles! Seize them!"

---

43 This word can mean either "a pit from which stone is extracted" (which would be the birthplace of the Gnargoyles) or "a prey animal caught by a predator" (which is what passes for "guest" on the Other Side).

CHAPTER SEVEN

(Three or Four Hours Left)[44]

*B*efore you even have a chance to use the S. Word for the first time, the Gnargoyles close in on you and Prince S. In a flurry of wings, stone, and intense gnarring, they grapple you with their industrial-strength, rock-hard muscles and pin your arms to your sides. They restrain you both from behind in what you can only describe as a reverse bear hug. They flap their massive wings and your feet lift off the beach. In a heartbeat,[45] you find yourself escorted by this dreadful cohort into the air at a dizzying speed.

FWOOP. FWOOP. FWOOP.

---

44 You still don't know if Prince S. was counting his thumb or not.
45 And your heart is beating pretty fast right now.

You can't escape. And your ears can't escape the sound of their stone wings chopping away at the fetid air. They lift you over the wall and you find yourself teetering above a dense city.

"Monstropolis!" the Gnargoyles roar, sounding like a chorus of the doomed singing their national anthem of despair.

A heavy blanket of soot hangs in the air. You wonder if this place has ever known the benefit of a single drop of rain. Filthy buildings tower like a forest of jagged teeth covered in glowing cavities. Only when your Gnargoyle captor swings you closer do you realize the holes are windows. Inside, you catch glimpses of terrifying monsters watching TV and doing their dishes.

Through the haze, you see winding streets and alleyways below that resemble a tangle of intestines carved from rock.[46] It all looks so primitive, it feels medieval, but medieval with electricity and cars. Green neon lights cast a hideous, eerie gleam into the night. They advertise all things monster: stench baths, growling lessons, tooth and claw sharpening. The horrid shops go on and on. With so many monstores, the citizens of Monstropolis must be big fans of commerce.[47]

---

46 Much like what a Gnargoyle's intestines are carved from
47 Money is the root of all evil, after all.

A bloodcurdling noise spews out of an enormous stadium ahead. The sound grows louder and more horrific as the Gnargoyles swoop toward it. But with your arms held hostage by your captor, you can do nothing to protect your ears. The Gnargoyles dive into the stadium and soar toward a large stage in the center.

Onstage, lit by a bright spotlight, you see three see-through women in flowing white gowns. They hover slightly above the stage. Each grips a microphone. They make that face singers make when belting out a high note—jaw quivering, eyes clenched shut, head thrown back in raw emotion—only the note is not a note, and they're not singing. They're punishing their audience with ear-destroying screeches. The roar of the crowd almost tops them, although it's unclear whether they roar in protest or enjoyment. In either case, you can't believe anyone would willingly attend such a concert.

FWOMP. You and your Gnargoyle captors land onstage. The transparent women glare at you with their bloodred eyes. Mercifully, your arrival ceases their shrieking.

The spotlight races over the crowd, revealing terrifying glimpses of the audience. The place teems with beasts, creatures, fiends, and horrors of every stripe and horn. Monsters. More than you can count. An undulating sea of fur, spiky tails, tentacles, and eyes on stalks. A nightmare's nightmare.

"What are you birdbrains doing?!" snaps one of the screechers. You're relieved to hear that her speaking voice doesn't sound nearly as distressing as her singing voice. "You dare interrupt the Banshee Band, One Night Only, Live at the Colosseum?"[48]

"Your show is over, Banshee!" shouts the Gnargoyle holding you. Of course it has to be the one to pick the fight.

---

48 Or, in their case, Undead at the Colosseum

The woman's face twists in rage as she brings her microphone to her mouth and emits another torturous wail. Her fellow Banshees follow suit. The Gnargoyles, champion shriekers themselves, emit their own blaring burst. This causes the Banshees to increase their volume. It sounds like a hundred competing dentist drills screaming inside your head, which is in danger of exploding if you don't put an end to this soon.

"STOP!" you scream as loud as you can. The wails and shrieks die off. A disturbing hush falls over the crowd. You know you weren't nearly as loud as the Banshees. Maybe it was just the sound of a real human's voice that made everyone stop screaming and take notice. You'd better think of something quick before any of the thousands of monsters watching you put it together that you are a real human.

Remembering the Gnargoyles' refrain on the beach, you wonder if you can't at least distract some of them for a minute with the suggestion of their favorite phrase. Desperate, you shout, "You know the law!"

"The law! The law! The law!" The Gnargoyles pick up your battle cry. You knew you could count on them. A murmur trickles through the crowd. "The law, the law, the law . . ." The chant grows rapidly and soon rains down upon the stage, the two words nearly indistinguishable as different sides of the stadium fail to synchronize. "Thelawthelawthelaw!" You stand there beneath the lights and your disguise, amazed for the second time at the level of passion and excitement these monsters have for the law. It must be no good.

"All right, all right." The lead Banshee raises her hands in the air, attempting to hush the crowd. When she realizes that her polite attempt has no effect at all, she lets out a soul-scorching screech. Smoke curls up off her microphone as she wails. The chanting dies down. She looks at your Gnargoyle captors. "You stupid stone bats! Of course we know the law."

The crowd erupts again in excitement.

Impatient, she shouts over them into her smoking microphone. "But we Banshees know the law will never come to pass. Listen to all of you mindless bunnies,[49] chanting away like Sunny Siders singing 'Happy Birthday'! No one will ever go to the Sunny Side. And no one will ever capture Prince S.!"

"Liar!" one of the Gnargoyles bellows. "It has been done! This monster here has captured Prince S."

---

49 Calling someone names that suggest gentleness, sweetness, or softness (like a bunny) is considered a major insult on the Other Side

She points her crooked finger at you. "You mean this thing here?" She cackles wildly and her backup Banshees join in. "I've never seen it before. I don't even know what it is!"

The spotlight finds you again. You feel the heat from its light and the weight of tens of thousands of monster eyeballs.

"Yes," you say, trying your best to sound like a monster while tamping down the nervous quiver in your voice. "I captured Prince S."

"I think you mean the Gnargoyles have captured you!" The Banshee squawks with laughter.

"No!" you shout. "Release me and Prince S."

To your surprise, the Gnargoyles comply. They shove Prince S. into the spotlight. The entire arena falls silent. The lack of sound feels even more deafening than all you have endured up to this point, possibly because your eardrums have been permanently damaged.

"Dear brethren of the Other Side," Prince S. begins.

"The Real Side!" something hollers from the crowd. You strain your eyes and see the source of the voice is a silver werewolf,[50] glinting in the moonlight.

---

50 Not to be confused with a silverware-wolf, which is a werewolf that turns into a piece of silverware every full moon. It's its own worst enemy.

Undaunted, Prince S. continues, "My captor here and I mean no harm, we simply wish to pass through unhindered."

Evil laughter simmers in the crowd and bubbles up into a river of raucous guffaws. The Banshee snickers into her microphone. "Pass through? How cute!" Her red eyes narrow. "You won't be passing through anywhere. Now that you're here, Prince S., you shall serve us for all time, not those sunburnt kittens and puppies above."

"Prince S. serves me!" you say, not entirely sure where you are going with this. "He stays with me wherever I go. And we're leaving now."

A murmur burbles through the crowd of concertgoers. The Banshee contorts her face in confusion. "But Prince S. must remain here!" she says. "He has not yet ripened into his wrongful mind. Only then will he and his dim-witted Couriers bring back stories from the real world where the villains are the heroes!"

The audience roars in approval. You can feel its collective breath buffeting your face like a hot, rotten wind, even under your disguise. No one here believes in toothbrushing.

"What?!" Prince S. gasps in disbelief.

"We demand equality!" a bucktoothed troll shouts from

the seats. "No longer will the people of the Real Side be treated as second-class citizens!"

"A world turned on its head?" Prince S. shouts. "Where good is evil and evil good? It makes no sense!"

"Oh, yes it does!" says the Banshee. "Think about it. We villains are always the ones who make the story worth telling. If it weren't for us, the goody-goody-two-shoes characters would just live out their pathetic lives without anything interesting happening to them."

"There would be no damsels in distress!" shouts a grizzled goblin.

"No cities burning to the ground!" bellows an eighty-foot lizard.

"No unexplained outbreaks of incurable diseases!" wheezes a mad scientist.

"Face it," says the Banshee. "Without us, there would be no stories. So, give us the respect we deserve. We should rule Astorya!"

The audience members clap and stomp their feet, hooves, and tentacles.

If I let them take Prince S., you think, *maybe they'll let me go. He'll be fine. He's fictional. I'm the one in danger. Besides, what has he ever done for me?*

No! you think. *That's my red voice again.*

Gritting your teeth beneath your disguise, you try to smother your red thoughts with happy memories. You think of Manteau, how he curls up on the pillow next to you at night, and how he insists the next morning that he doesn't snore. You feel your red voice retreat.

A flare of evil-smelling smoke explodes next to you. From out of the foul cloud steps what looks like an ordinary businessman. But then you see he has a tail and a pair of curved horns crowning his head. Greased up with enough oil to power a small city, his perfectly combed hair shines in the spotlight. His tail dances behind him like a cobra preparing to attack.

"Dear Heavens," groans Prince S. "The Politician-Magician. I could have guessed that unctuous[51] scoundrel would be at the core of this villainous law."

The horned man wrenches the microphone from the Banshee's transparent fist and flashes the crowd a cheesy smile.

"Let's all give another hand to the Banshee Band!" he says in a voice as smooth as polished silver. "One of Monstropolis's worst groups." The monster masses shower the stage with applause. This seems to appease the Banshees. As the audience calms down, he turns to Prince S. and purrs into the microphone, "Welcome to our foul city, Your Highness. We built it with the hopes that you would one day see it, and now here you are."

He turns his red eyes on you. "We thank you for doing your civic duty," he says. "Now that we have Prince S., we'll never let him go." He chuckles smugly to himself.

The red rings in Prince S.'s eyes flash. "You scullion!" he snarls at the oil vat on two legs. "You boil! You nameless

---

51 This word can either mean "full of false flattery" or "oily" (or, in this case, both).

knave! Let me go at once, you plague-sore!"

"Flattery will get you a one-way ticket to my penthouse at the Tower of Wrath," the Politician-Magician says and snaps his fingers. A sudden burst of smoke envelops Prince S.

"Prince S.?" you call out, reaching into the cloud. As the smoke clears, you realize you claw at nothing. Prince S. has vanished. "What did you do to Prince S.?" you scream.

"Don't worry," laughs the Politician-Magician. "He'll be safe and sound until he's seeing red, and much less agreeable the next time you see him. Now, we all know the law . . ."

"The law . . . the law . . ." A new chant catches on in the crowd.

"Whoever among us can complete the impossible task of crossing over to the Sunny Side and bringing back Prince S. shall become our new leader."

Their new leader? So this is the law? Maybe you can use your new status to your advantage.

"That's right!" you attempt to growl. "I'm your new leader. Now bring Prince S. back."

"Not so fast." The Politician-Magician wags a greasy finger at you. "The law clearly states on page six hundred sixty-six . . ." He snaps his fingers and another puff of smoke, reeking of a grease fire, appears. Inside it floats a thick stack of papers, no doubt the document upon which the law that seems to obsess everyone in this town is written. ". . . that before assuming office, the new leader shall first have the duty and pleasure of personally dismantling our city council, monster by monster. So, everyone ready for a neck-snapping good time?"

"I'd have a good time snapping your neck!" The words fly out of your mouth. Hearing them shocks you. You would never say anything like that! But the red voice in your head must have hijacked your tongue. Your rightful mind knows for certain that the words "neck-snapping" and "good time" don't belong anywhere near each other.

"Sounds like you're ready," he says with a grin.

"No!" you say. "Bring back Prince S.!"

"I'd be happy to obey that command," he says, "once you officially become our new leader. But first, you have to defeat our current administration. Sorry, my hands are tied. The law is the law."

"The law is the law!" the Gnargoyles bellow behind you.

You consider ripping off your disguise so you can grab your pencil. But as he demonstrated with Prince S., this guy can make things happen with just a snap of his fingers. You wouldn't have a chance to write a word before he disarmed you, or worse.

As if he somehow knew you were thinking about him snapping his fingers, the Politican-Magician snaps his fingers. In his signature poof of smoke, he disappears from the stage. All that remains of him is the stench of burnt grease and a puddle of oil where he stood.

"Now that's a much better view," the Politician-Magician's silky voice booms out of the loudspeakers. "Our soon-to-be leader looks even smaller from up here!" Then he makes his voice sound like one of those sports announcers who stretch out every word into practically its own song. "Geeeeet readyyyyyy, Monstropoliiiiis, foooor the greaaaatest showdooooown everrrrrrrrrrrr!"

The crowd cheers ferociously. The Gnargoyles and the Banshees lift off like a flock of birds sensing danger, leaving you alone on the stage. A cheesy theme song of synthesized horns and thumping drums blasts out of the loudspeakers. Your heart thumps along with it.

So this is how Monstropolis does democracy.

CHAPTER EIGHT

(Three-Something Hours Left, or maybe
even less time, who knows?)

*T*he stadium lights flicker on, flooding the arena. Once your eyes adjust, you see that the stage you stand on sits like an island in the center of a sea of dirt. Or, more accurately, a gladiator ring.

"Now," the voice of the Politician-Magician echoes throughout the stadium, "where are our city council members? I'm sure some of you came out tonight to see the Banshee Band. Come on, don't be shy. Who'll be the first to take on the monster who captured Prince S., the fiercest, the foulest, the most dangerous monster of all monsterdom?"

"Tee-hee!" rings out a teeny-weeny, high-pitched voice.

"Me!" The voice sounds cutesy, small, and sweet, like the kind of voice you would imagine belonging to a fun-size candy bar. Your spirits lift. You feel like you could handle a monster that sounds like that.

"I'd recognize that voice anywhere," says the Politician-Magician.

A spotlight skirts through the audience and shines on what looks like a heap of milky bricks.

"Yay, yay, let's play!" giggles the voice. Your eyes graze the crest of the heap, searching for some wee, sweet treat to appear on top, but none comes. Instead, the rocky pile itself rises, and your heart sinks.

"Representing the junk food and possessed objects of our foul city, he's forty feet tall and deadly sweet—it's the Big Rock Candy Mountain Man!" announces the Politician-Magician. The crowd rejoices ferociously.

In spite of his puny, syrupy voice, this civic leader of Monstropolis happens to be a giant. A giant apparently made of rock candy and holding a wooden club the size of a mature oak tree. Or maybe it's not a club, but an actual oak tree he ripped out of the ground.

The Big Rock Candy Mountain Man stomps his way down the stands toward you. Hideous crunches and wails erupt from the audience members he crushes along the

way. Frozen in terror, you can't take your eyes away from the monster as he crashes through the front row and thunders into the ring. You take in a deep breath of the foul air.

"Yum, yum, here I come!" he squeals in his sugary voice. Towering over you, the Big Rock Candy Mountain Man raises his arm and shakes his fist. Chunks of rock candy slough[52] off him and rain down around you like sugar meteors.

You remind yourself that your monster disguise is invincible. But then you realize the fatal flaw in your design. Your disguise may be invincible, but you're not. What if the giant steps on you? Your fictional costume may survive, but what about your very real bones and soft tissues?

Now would be a good time to run.

You dart toward the back of the stage, zigging and zagging to dodge the deadly candy dandruff. The Big Rock Candy Mountain Man heaves his giant club high above his head and smashes it down onto the stage, which splits in half with a tremendous *CRRRRACK*! You tumble onto the dirt below.

---

52 To shed or remove. Rhymes with "stuff," not to be confused with Slough, which rhymes with "now," a town west of London, England (not London, Ohio).

The arena ring offers nothing in the way of cover. And the walls, too tall to climb, encircle the entire arena, giving you no hope of escape. Although, judging by the gory and gruesome faces in the stands, the audience might be more dangerous than the Big Rock Candy Mountain Man. So, left with no other options, you run as the giant lumbers after you, hurling deadly bits of himself all the while. The Monstropolitans boo and hiss (especially the snake monsters).

"Very clever!" the voice of the Politician-Magician rings out. "Looks like our would-be leader is trying to exhaust the Big Rock Candy Mountain Man. Too bad the Big Rock Candy Mountain Man never runs out of energy—he's on a permanent sugar rush!"

You didn't have any real plan when you started running away, aside from staying alive. But hearing the news that your giant adversary won't ever tire makes your exhausted limbs feel even more heavy. You push onward, though, completing your first hopeless lap around the massive grounds.

"Wheeee!" You hear the Big Rock Candy Mountain Man exuding childlike gleevil.[53] "Runsies-funsies!" You wonder

---

53 Gleeful evil

who would write such a twisted character, and why.

Owww! You trip over a rock candy rock and belly flop onto the dirt. *SPLOOOFFF!*

"Hope you had a nice trip!" the Politician-Magician snickers. The crowd breaks out in monstrous laughter. Laughing at the misfortune of others must be one of the few pleasures they allow themselves in their miserable lives. It certainly couldn't be from the quality of his joke.

Winded, your whole body clenches in pain. You roll over and lift your head. The candy colossus coming to candy-crush you looks even bigger than before.

You reach for your pencil, but your monster hand finds something else instead. The scabbard of the S. Word! You forgot you had tied it around your waist. But didn't Prince S. say not to use the S. Word? But what choice do you have? You've never used the S. Word before. You don't know how much damage it could inflict on a creature made of rock candy. Can he even feel pain?

You know you can feel pain, and that's all the motivation you need.

Hoisting yourself back onto your feet, you grab the hilt of the S. Word. The gleaming sword leaps out of its sheath and jams itself firmly into your monster hand with a *SCHWING!*

When you try to lift the sword, it weaves wildly. The S. Word slashes at the air in broad strokes, as if it were writing a secret message in invisible letters. Probably a plea to Prince S. to return to it. Is it possessed? Has the Other Side turned it evil? The S. Word has a will of its own. It's like someone attached a wild animal to your hand.

"Innnnnteresting . . . ," says the Politician-Magician. "Using the S. Word. Must have picked it up from Prince S."

The S. Word lunges, causing you to lurch forward. *What is it doing?* It takes another stab at the air, yanking you toward the oncoming Big Rock Candy Mountain Man.

What was Prince S.'s warning? *Don't use the S. Word. Listen to it.* The sword seems to want to drag you closer to the Big Rock Candy Mountain Man. That's the last place you want to be. But you can't keep running forever, especially if he can. The S. Word jabs the air. It seems to be telling you to charge.

Listen to the S. Word.

With no other options, you run toward the Big Rock Candy Mountain Man, screaming. To the spectators, your scream may seem like the frenzied battle cry of a fearless warrior, but you know the truth: You're terrified.

You charge right between the giant's lumbering legs. As

he grinds to a halt, you swing the S. Word at his ankle. But the blade skews off in the opposite direction. You can't believe you missed such an enormous target. You swear the S. Word itself messed it up for you. Since it seems to want to go that way, you take a hacking whack at the other ankle. It veers away, making you miss again. Angered, you hold the hilt to your lips and growl, "If you want to see Prince S. again, you gotta work with me here!"

The blade shakes in your hand, as if it were saying NO. Maybe it's trying to tell you something. Maybe it doesn't want you to strike the giant's leg. Maybe it won't do any damage, or worse, maybe it'll break the S. Word.

The giant shifts his enormous feet and swats at you. The S. Word jerks, pulling you out of the way of his pulverizing palm. He leans over to get a better look at the pesky nuisance at his heels. The second his face appears between his legs, the S. Word quivers. *Now!* You ram the blade into one of his red eyes.

"Ouchies!!!" the giant screams[54] in a pitch that makes the werewolves in the stadium howl. As he reels back, the S. Word slips out of your grip and remains lodged in his eye.

"Looks like he sees the point!" says the Politician-Magician.

---

54 Looks like he can feel pain after all.

The giant staggers around the arena, tearing at his face, struggling to extract the S. Word from his eye with his giant fingers, like a person trying to remove a splinter while wearing mittens. You dart away from his enormous trampling feet.

"We knew this wasn't going to be a fair fight," says the Politician-Magician, "but I'm sure our almost-new leader would appreciate a bigger challenge. Who else is here from the city council?"

A hideous gurgle burbles up from somewhere in the audience. Cheers tear through the crowd. Your body—and the entire stadium—vibrates from all the hollering.

"Well, look who it is!" says the Politician-Magician. "I thought I smelled her out there. Representing scum, pollution, and gelatinous cubes, she's contaminated our city since we laid the first stone. You know her, you hate her, put your appendages together for Hazmata, Empress of Ooze!"

You rip your eyes away from the stumbling giant. The spotlight lands on a repulsive blob—what can only be the Empress of Ooze. The monsters on either side of her shove each other out of the way as she seeps down the stands. Screams echo through the stadium as she singes over the spectators in her path.

"Watch out, folks!" says the Politician-Magician. "Hazmata can melt your face right off. Which may be an improvement for some of you!"

"Ahhhh!" the giant sighs, his voice full of relief as he finally plucks the S. Word out of his eye. He flicks it away. Your eyes follow the sword as it whips through the air, all the way to the other end of the arena, and stabs into the ground. Not far from it, Hazmata drips off the edge of the stands and congeals on the arena floor. If you don't move quickly, she'll cut off your path to the S. Word.

The Big Rock Candy Mountain Man looks down at you with his one good eye and says, "No more Mr. Nicey-Wicey." His words may sound cutesy, but his intention is deadly-weadly. You make a break for it just as he swings his club at you. Wind gusts at your back as it passes behind you. Lucky for you, you wrecked his depth perception when you stabbed his eye. His club smashes into the stands, sending spectators flying. The rest of the audience clamors for more.

You race across the arena as fast as your monster feet can take you. Hazmata slithers into your path. You try to keep your eyes on the S. Word, but it's hard to look away from her hideousness.[55] She looks like a cross between

---

55 "Her Hideousness" also happens to be what her subjects call her.

a vast wobbling dollop of gray-green goop and a baby pool full of jiggling pus. But if you find her appearance repulsive, her stench practically knocks you into the next world. The closer you get, the more her stink fills your mouth with the flavor of someone else's festering vomit—which is way worse to have in your mouth than your own—topped with sweaty underwear (also someone else's). You gag.

"Goingh somewherghe?" she garbles[56] at you. You dodge to the right, out of her path, and barrel toward the S. Word.

"Time for smashy-bashy!" The giant continues to make violence sound like an activity for kindergartners. With his thunderous footfalls drawing closer, you sprint over to the sword and yank it out of the ground. The crowd bays in delight as you spin around to face your foes.

Hazmata spreads her

---

56 To get an idea of what Hazmata sounds like, try to talk while gargling pudding (make sure to wear a bib).

mucoid body out in both directions, forming a quivering, gel-like wall around you. The Big Rock Candy Mountain Man towers behind her. The wall of the arena stands at your back and the monsters have you cornered. You grip the S. Word with both hands, praying that it will save you, but it makes no move. Maybe it doesn't see a way out of this position, either.

"Shaaygh ghoodbyeghh!" Hazmata says. She slops a massive goober of her homegrown goo through the air at you. To your surprise, the S. Word rears back, pulling you with it and twisting you into the stance of a baseball player at bat.

Looks like the S. Word wants you to play ball. But in this case, it's one strike and you're out.

Hazmata's globule flies toward you. You turn the blade so the flat side faces out and swing it like a major-league slugger. *SPLACK!* You hit it! It sails over Hazmata and into the giant's leg. Home run! The audience goes wild.

"Double ouchies!" the giant cries. Hazmata's ball of acidic goo burrows into his leg, leaving a smoking hole. He stares at his widening wound as more of his leg melts away. The smell of caramel fills the air, which adds a nice counterpoint to Hazmata's stench. The Big Rock Candy Mountain Man crumples and topples over.

KRRRRRRSHHHHHH!!!

The giant collides with the ground behind the wall of Hazmata. A plume of sugar and dirt showers you.

The wall of Hazmata closes in. If she touches you, you're toast.[57] You have to get over her somehow.

From his downed position, the giant raises his club. *The club!* you think. It's risky, but you might be able to hitch a ride on the giant's club. Ideally, without it crushing you.

"Over here, one-eye!" you taunt the Big Rock Candy Mountain Man. He takes the bait and swings his club at you. You leap out of the way just in time. His club smashes down on the ground beside you.

Now's your chance! Before he lifts the club again, you press your body against it and hold on for dear life. He raises it for another attack, taking you with it. You nearly lose your lunch on the ride up.

"Where'd you go?" he asks in his puny voice.

"Yough fooughl!" Hazmata gargle-screams.

From atop the club, you see Hazmata below, recoiling like a gooey rubber band, snapping out of her wall shape and reconstituting herself back into a slime heap. The giant scans the arena, searching for you. Before he realizes

---

57 And not the kind you have with butter and jam

where you are, you scramble down the club, onto his arm, and jump onto the ground.

"Well, look who it is!" says the Politician-Magician. "Representing disastrous weather events and relentless greed, let's give a warm welcome to our city council treasurer, Glacie the Ice Dragon!"

You look up and see an enormous blue dragon barreling down from the heavens toward the arena. This isn't your day.

Tearing your eyes away from the dragon, you see Hazmata slew[58] closer to you. It's remarkable how quickly she moves without any legs. "Thigghs endsgh nowgh!!!" She quivers in gelatinous fury, piling herself higher.

Above her head, the dragon opens her terrible jaws. "Time to freeze your assets." Her wicked voice resounds through the arena. A blue flame blazes in her mouth.

You try to run, but the S. Word jerks you back. What is it trying to tell you? You probably couldn't outrun this dragon's death-breath anyway. But what else can you do?

The memory of Prince S. fighting the Rubots in Rulette's castle hits you like a smack in the forehead. By spinning the blade, he deflected the Rubots' lasers back at them.

---

58 A violent sliding movement, also the past tense of "slay" (which is what she intends to do to you)

It's worth a try. You attempt the maneuver, passing the hilt over and under your awkward monster hands. The S. Word must agree with your strategy, because in spite of your fumbling, it spins in a perfect circle like a fan on the highest setting.

Hazmata wobbles in preparation for what will almost certainly be the last thing you see. At the same time, Glacie the Ice Dragon unleashes her breath. A blistering wind blasts out of her mouth. You close your eyes and grit your teeth behind the spinning blade of the S. Word. The howl of icy gales drowns your ears.

The S. Word slows to a halt in your hands. You crack your eyes open. The arena has been transformed into a winter wonderland. A blanket of blue-white ice coats the ground. Icicles hang from the stands. The front row of monsters look like snowmen with evil red eyes. And a few feet in front of you, Hazmata sits like a Christmas tree made of frozen puke. Mercifully, the ice has encapsulated her smell, as well.

But you remain unfrozen. The spinning mirror move shielded you from Glacie's arctic blast! Your heart sings an ode of gratitude to Prince S.'s marvelous blade. But the ode ends abruptly when your ear picks up the muffled sound of a jackhammer nearby. *What now?* You brace yourself, as you doubt you can handle yet another attack. A few yards away, the ice starts to crack and a power tool emerges, followed by an adorable vole in a hard hat. He looks super cute until he turns his red eyes on you.

"Howdy!" he squeaks. "You ready to die?"

"Oooo!" says the Politician-Magician. "The most explosive member of our city council has made it to the party! Give it up for Volecano!"

The crowd roils with excitement. "VOLE-CANE-OH! VOLE-CANE-OH!"

Volecano waves at his adoring fans. High above, you see the dragon circling around to make another pass.

Still nestled in the hole he made in the ice, he scrunches his face up tight and balls his fists. He starts to shake and so does the ground. You widen your stance to keep from falling over. Judging by his name, he's brewing up some kind of volcanic eruption. You've got to stop him.

Forgetting the ice, you run toward him. And slip. And slide feetfirst along the ground into a slushy patch of mud. Tendrils of steam curl up from the ground. All around you, the ice melts. You don't have much time. Getting to your feet, you slosh your way over to him.

You thought for sure he would disappear down his hole

or spring out and fight you. Instead, he remains half out of his hole, quivering and straining. His eyes pinched shut. Paws clenched. Teeth grinding.

A terrible rumble reverberates through the ground. You reach down and grab the vole. He fits snugly inside your monster hand, his body still quaking.

VOOMP!

VOOMP!

The sound of approaching wings startles you. You turn in time to see the Ice Dragon plunging straight at you. Her red eyes burn with vengeful determination. She opens her cavernous mouth. Without hesitation, you chuck Volecano at her. Volecano, still transfixed, flies through the air and sails right into her throat.

"Vole in one!" the Politician-Magician announces.

The audience loves it. They hoot and applaud as Glacie the Ice Dragon buckles in the air and crashes to the arena floor. She convulses, choking on Volecano. Her stumpy arms are too short to give herself any variation of the Heimlich maneuver; she has no choice but to full-body heave like a cat coughing up a hair ball.[59] It might be your imagination, but she looks a little bluer now. Maybe from the oxygen deprivation. Or maybe ice dragons get bluer the more enraged they become.

Volecano must still be orchestrating his volcano from within the Ice Dragon's throat, because the ground continues to steam and shake. Beyond the choking dragon, Hazmata jiggles the icicles off her globulous body. The arm of the Big Rock

---

59 Volecano is, in a sense, a hair ball.

Candy Mountain Man lifts out of the melting snowdrift where he lies, club still in hand, and slams down on the ground again.

"Looks like it's time for round two," the Politician-Magician says.

You've got to get out of here. You look down at Volecano's hole. That must lead somewhere. And anywhere is better than here. It's narrow, but you might be able to squeeze through.

You lower your legs inside, but that's as far as you get. The hole just can't accommodate you, especially in your unwieldly monster disguise. You will have to take it off. Without another thought, you pry your legs out of the hole and rip off your monster costume, letting it fall to the ground. You feel overwhelmed with relief to be free of your cumbersome disguise.

Then you remember you are standing in front of a stadium packed with monsters. The entire crowd gasps.

"It's"—the Politician-Magician chokes on his words—"a human?!"

Voices cry out from the stands:

"Get it!"

"Destroy it!"

"Eat it!"

"Save some for me!"

Monsters pour down the walls and onto the trembling ground of the arena, trampling one another in their mania to do unspeakable things to you. As if you needed more of an invitation to flee, the Ice Dragon finally upchucks Volecano and turns her red eyes on you. "You'll pay for this!" she hisses. Before she can make you into a snow cone, you grab the S. Word and slide down into the Volecano hole.

Even without your disguise, it's a tight fit. Wedged between jagged rocks, you frantically wriggle your body downward. Pebbles drop onto your head as the ground continues to quake. The tunnel walls grow hotter. Your heart bludgeons your chest as you hear the murderous horde stampeding nearer. You spelunk[60] down farther, farther, farther, until the light from the arena no longer reaches you. In the darkness, you hear monsters scrape at the hole above you.

The rumble of the quaking earth drowns out all else. You brace yourself against the sharp rocks. A crack forms

---

60 To explore a cave (usually done as a relaxing hobby, not while fleeing a stadium full of monsters)

at your feet. A whisper of eerie light trickles through. You kick at it and a chunk falls away. More light seeps in. You kick and kick until the hole grows large enough for you to squeeze through and drop down.

CLOOM. Your feet strike the floor of what looks like a drainage pipe, sending a haunting echo of your landing down the tube. Fluorescent lighting flickers overhead, casting the pipe in a green-gray gloom. Slimy, shiny mold coats the walls. What smells like the odor of one thousand old-man armpits (the kind of geezers who have given up showering and changing their shirts) rushes into your nostrils. But you will take this funk any day over Hazmata's company.

The ground continues to shake. You run. Even though the tremors increase with every step you take, even though the slick slime under your feet makes you slip, even though you have no idea what might await you at the end of this tunnel, you press on. You have to get as much distance as you can from the impending—

KA-BOOOOOM!!!

CHAPTER NINE

(Two Hours Left?)

*L*uckily, you miss Volecano's big finish. You certainly wouldn't have survived it. And don't feel sorry for the spectators who were trying to murder you. They'll be fine. While a volcano erupting in a packed stadium would normally be a tragedy beyond measure, it's a cause for celebration when the stadium is packed with monsters. No one loves disaster more than the monsters of Monstropolis. It doesn't hurt that fictional beings cannot actually be destroyed in a lasting way by the lava or the collapse of the Colosseum or any other physical trauma. What would finish you off in an excruciating manner would merely entertain them. In fact, this night will go down in the Monstropolis history books as the best

Banshee Band concert of all time.

But your plan to escape by using Volecano's tunnel has one significant drawback. Lava, like all liquid, flows down, not up. So after it spurts out into the arena, it spills into your escape tunnel.

You don't have to glance over your shoulder to know the molten menace has entered the pipe, but you do anyway. The lava plops in steaming drops from the hole you kicked open, sizzling away the rot. It begins to snake through the pipe behind you.[61]

You run. It's much easier to run now that you are free of your monster costume. But you can't help but notice that each time your foot hits the pipe, it sounds like the word *doom*. *DOOM, DOOM, DOOM, DOOM*. Doom follows your every step. Since Astorya is such a literal place, you hope that doesn't mean your real doom is upon you. Though, from the heat pressing on your back, you know that the lava is close on your heels.

As if navigating these horrid-smelling, dimly lit pipes wasn't enough of a challenge, now you must flee free-flowing fire,[62] as well. At least this lava doesn't move quite as fast as rushing water. Therein lies most of your hope of outrunning it. But it does move, and unlike water, touching

---

61 At least the lava should take care of the mold problem.
62 For an extra challenge, try saying "flee free-flowing fire" three times fast.

it will
cause
fatal
damage.

Your feet fly
faster. You almost
slide right into a hole in
the floor, but you manage
to skid to a stop beforehand.
If you jump over this hole and
keep running, the hole may divert
enough of the lava down to stanch the
flow following you, or at least cut it back.

You leap over the hole and hurry forward.
Looking back, you watch as the lava pours down
into the hole. You feel greatly relieved. That takes
some of the pressure off, but you dare not tarry too long,
as Prince S. would say. If only he were here with you now.
Even with his infuriating memory problems and overblown
manner of speech, you miss him. But any hope of finding
him will have to wait until you find a way out of here. Before
you turn to go, you watch in horror as the lava fills up the
hole and continues to flow down the pipe toward you. Panic
replaces your relief.

What you don't realize is that you've entered
Monstropolis's sewer system. Since it was built by monsters,
it doesn't function that well as a sewer, but it excels as
a confounding maze of pipes. Everything connects to

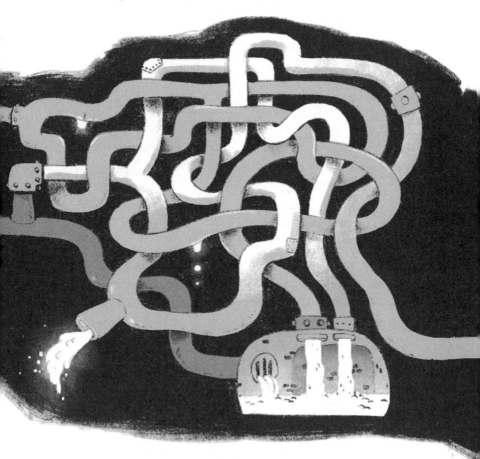

everything else, so the lava will eventually fill the entire
system. You must find the exit and find it fast, keeping in
mind that you may have to go down to go up, as well as keep

a constant lookout for the marauding molten fire.

You tumble forward and slide down a series of elbow joints, bashing your own elbows and other body parts against the sides of the pipe as you go. BONK. (Your head.) BINK. (Your tailbone.) CLANK. (The S. Word.) If this were a ride at a water park, it would be the one with the shortest line. The bumpy, abusive journey ends with you in yet another pipe.

You bring yourself back to your feet, dash ahead, and
soon come to a bend in the pipe. It looks like you have no
choice but to climb down. Grateful to have the use of your
real hands again, you climb down the slimy metal rungs
only to find yourself standing in a nearly identical pipe
to the one you just left. Gray-green fluorescent lighting,

mold as wallpaper, nauseating stench, and completely disgusting—the main difference here being that this pipe doesn't have lava in it. *Yet*, you remind yourself.

A sizzling hiss behind you announces the arrival of the lava. That didn't take long. You sprint through the pipe with the lava in pursuit till you round a corner, only to see lava also coming at you from the other direction. A fresh crop of sweat breaks out on your brow and not just from the heat. You backtrack, scouring the pipe for another way out. You find an opening above you, but you can't reach it. The idea of writing yourself a jet pack or a flying carpet flashes across your mind, but with the steaming streams slithering toward you from both sides, you will be barbecued before you finish a single sentence.

Your eye catches the glint of rungs in the wall and you realize there must be a ladder hidden under the mold. Raking at it, you scrape away the slime until you can get your fingers around the rung. You hoist yourself up just as the lava streams meet below your feet. The heat practically melts your fictional footwear. You dig into the next rung and clamber up. The mold doesn't make matters easier, but if you just take it nice and slow, you won't—

Slip.

You tumble backward toward the smoldering river below. As you fall, the S. Word catches on one of the rungs. You find yourself dangling with your feet inches above the rising tide of liquid fire. Saved by the S. Word once again. It hasn't failed you yet.

Your fingers claw onto the moldy rung above you, and you swing your feet back onto the rungs. As carefully as you can while hyperventilating with fear, you climb. Up the pipe you go until you reach the last rung. It's a dead end. *Dead* being a little too on the nose, considering the rising lava below you. The temperature inside the pipe continues to rise as well. You feel feverish. The lava makes red and orange lights dance all around you. They look beautiful. Still, you don't want them to be the last thing you see.

Frantically, you scrape the ceiling of the pipe. Stalactites of mold splinter off and fall in your face. Your finger finds a divot in the mold. It's not over yet! Crazy with desperation, you claw at the mold and excavate a familiar shape. "It's a wheel!" You laugh uncontrollably, madness tugging at your mind. You hook one arm onto a rung and turn the wheel with your free hand. It groans and creaks, resistant to your advances, but you possess the strength of a maniac on the cusp of death. "Come on!" you scream at the wheel, wrenching it with all your might.

CLUNK.

The hatch opens as the lava almost laps at your feet. You scramble up and through the hole, close the hatch behind you, and twist it shut.

You collapse in relief, hardly noticing your new surroundings. You wouldn't be able to notice them anyway—it's pitch dark.

Something with lots of little legs scurries over the nape of your neck. "Aagh!" You flail to your feet, swatting at your neck and shoulders. A moment passes. You run your fingers under your collar and brush off your shirt, but don't find any creepy-crawlies. Must have been your imagination. Maybe.

"Are you afraid of the dark?" a voice whispers. You freeze. Someone—or something—is in here with you. Wherever "here" is. You don't dare answer. You're afraid to even breathe. "Or is it just bugs?" the voice asks. "You afraid of bugs? Then I got bad news for you."

CLICK.

A light snaps on. You drop into a wide stance, tensing your body, ready for an attack. But none comes. Whipping your head left and right, you scan the room for the source of the voice. But you see no one. A cheap-looking lamp glows from atop a large and badly scratched wooden desk. Papers sprawl in haphazard piles. Discarded coffee cups litter the room. The corpse of a half-eaten doughnut lies in repose on the grimiest carpet you've ever laid eyes on.

"That one was free," the voice says. "Just a sample of some of the scares I got in store for ya."

"What?" you say, completely confused.

"Scares," the voice repeats. Her accent has a real New York City quality—a little gruff, a little hurried, and a lot in the know—like someone who doesn't have the time for small talk, but could talk to you for a week straight about nothing in particular. "Isn't that why you're here? What else would ya be doing in my office?"

"No," you say. "I'm . . ." You hesitate, not sure if you should reveal anything to this invisible tormentor. "I was just escaping the lava."

"Oh, Volecano's still flogging that old routine, eh? Well, gotta give the people what they like."

"Yeah . . . ," you say to the empty room. "Where are you? Are you a ghost?"

"Are you a comedian?" she asks. "You're looking right at me! Don't tell me ya never heard of the Fearmonger. Phobia the Fearmonger?"

You don't want to offend her, but she must glean from your expression that you have never heard of Phobia the Fearmonger

"Ugh!" she says. "What am I spending all that money on advertising for? Ya never heard my jingle?"

She clears her throat and belts out a little tune:

"For a real good scare
That'll raise your hair
Don't wait any longer
Call the Fearmonger!"

Wincing, you shake your head no. Even Banjoe couldn't write a song that bad.

"Ah, who am I kidding?" she says in despair. "Look at this dump. I tell ya, it's a tough gig, selling scares to monsters. They don't scare easy. But that doesn't mean I don't have top-of-the-line scares for you. Hold on, take a seat, let me get my brochure."

Off to the side, you see a sad excuse for a chair. The way she said for you to take it, you feel like you have to, even though you really don't have time for this kind of thing. Whatever it is. You have to find Prince S., hide the original Original, and get back to the Sunny Side before this place ruins you. Just as you lower yourself into the dilapidated chair, you see a glossy brochure herk and jerk itself to the middle of the desk. A little cockroach pokes out from underneath the brochure. Instinctively, you raise your hand to smack it.

"Whoa, whoa, whoa!" The cockroach rears up and waves her front legs. So she's the one who has been talking to you. "What is it with you people? No respect at all for other life. So violent! You know, I've known a lot of monsters. Really sick, mean, low-down, evil monsters. The best of the worst. But you humans take the cake. Speaking of cake, I got some nice ten-month-old cake around here somewhere if you're interested."

"No," you say. "Thanks."

"All right, all right, no cake, let's get right to it. Take a look at my brochure."

With great hesitation, you pick up the brochure. As you read the words on the front page, you hear the cockroach's voice-over shouting at you,[63] "Phobia the Fearmonger, guaranteed fright or half your money back!"

You try to put it back on the desk, but it sticks to your hand.

"Hey, careful with my brochure. I only got one."

"Sorry," you say as you manage to flick it onto the desk.

"So, what do I need to do to get you into a scare today? No matter what you're scared of, I got it. Nothing's too

---

63 As with all things written in Astorya, you hear the author's voice reading aloud while you read it.

creepy, nothing's too weird. I don't judge. I even got a scare that's one hundred percent guaranteed to work. I call it the Scarea. 'Cuz it's a scary area. And it'll scare ya. Get it? It works on two levels. Scarea. I'm good at making up names. Anyway, every single monster I've sold it to, and some of them have been the evilest in town, can't even bring themselves to go near it. It's that scary."

"What is it?" you ask.

"How am I to know? It's too scary to get close enough to see!"

The gears turn in your mind. A place that even the evilest monsters won't go near. That could be the place that Prince S. was talking about, the perfect hiding spot for the original Original.

"I'll take it," you say.

"All right." Phobia takes a long look at you. "Ten thousand pieces of filthy lucre."

"What?" you say.

"Ya know, moola, shmoola, the means, the mazuma, the wherewithal, specie, shekels, pelf, dough, bread, greens, cheddar."

You can't be sure, but it sounded like the cockroach started ordering lunch at the end of her sentence.

"You mean money?" you ask.

"Give the kid a cigar!" she cheers.

"Okay, I can give you money," you say, reaching for your pencil and paper.

"Hold on!" she barks. "Did I say ten thousand? I meant twenty."

"Fine."

"No, wait!" She stops you again. "Did I say twenty thousand? I meant twenty hundred thousand."

"Sure."

"Twenty hundred thousand thousand."

"Whatever you want," you say, pulling out your pencil.

"I don't take checks!" she says. "Cash only. Filthy lucre."

"Don't worry," you say.

"You really got twenty hundred thousand thousand on you? Do you realize how many zeroes that is? If you're trying to do the math on your paper there, that's twenty times a hundred thousand times a thousand. That's two billion smackeroonies. I got a mind for numbers."

While Phobia blathers on about her mathematical abilities, you set about pretending to make your own calculations (no need to alert her to your superpower), while actually writing her money instead:

Twenty hundred thousand thousand pieces of filthy lucre make a pile on Phobia's desk right now.

A deluge of golden coins showers down, quickly burying Phobia, her lamp, her desk, and most of her office. The lucre comes all the way up to your lap. For the record, these two billion pieces of filthy lucre happen to be the cleanest money in all of Monstropolis, mostly because they were not gained in a dishonorable way. Although technically, one could argue that they are counterfeit. But if they are counterfeit, they are no more counterfeit than anything else in this fictional world.

"Are you okay?" you ask as you try to excavate the Fearmonger from the pile of money.

A very muffled "I'm great!" squeaks out from beneath the coins. She wriggles out from under them and scuttles up to the top of the pile, her tiny red eyes burning bright with money madness. "This is quite a chunk of change here! After this gig, I can retire." She takes a deep whiff of the coins. "Mmmm-mmm-mmmm! Smells fresh! Gotta love money, it's the root of all evil.[64] Just marvelous!"

Before she has a chance to question how you produced

---

64 We told you so.

so much cash so fast, you change the subject.

"I need help with something else," you say.

"Anything you want," she says, "free of charge."

"I need to find my friend. The Politician-Magician has him somewhere called the Penthouse of Doom or Rage or something."

"The Tower of Wrath. Must be an important friend. The Politician-Magician only abducts the best. Your friend got a name?"

"Prince S."

"Prince S. as in *the* Prince S.?! You gotta be kidding me!"

"No, he's really Prince S."

"And the Politician-Magician has him?"

An oily poof of smoke erupts in the air and a letter floats down, landing on top of the money pile. The Fearmonger darts over to it.

"Speak of the devil!" she exclaims. She squirms her little cockroach body under the seal, opens the envelope, and drags out a very formal-looking invitation. "Take a look at this!"

You lean closer and read the cursive written in ink as red as blood (at least you hope it's ink):

You are nefariously invited to:
The Wickeding of Prince S.
In one hour's time
The Politician-Magician's Tower of Wrath
Sinister Ballroom
Black tie violently enforced

The voice-over of the Politican-Magician purrs out the words on the invitation. You can practically feel the oil dripping down your eardrums.

"How do you like that?" The Fearmonger cackles. "I become a billionaire and thirty seconds later, I get invited to the most exclusive gala event in the history of Monstropolis. All the most ruthless and powerful monsters will be there. I'm moving up in the world! Now, what am I gonna wear? Hold on."

As Phobia slips into a drawer, you slip into your thoughts. You have to assume "the Wickeding" means the moment Prince S. becomes evil. So you only have an hour to get to this event, rescue Prince S., reach the Scarea, and then somehow get back to the Sunny Side. Never mind that the crowd attending Prince S.'s doom will likely pose a far greater threat to you than the Colosseum full of monsters. Your heart rattles with anxiety. Also, you have nothing to wear.

At least you can do something about that last worry. With Phobia still rummaging deep in her wardrobe (which she apparently keeps in her desk drawer), you grab your pencil and dream up the fanciest clothes possible for yourself. You decide to top off your whole outfit with a mask, as you wouldn't want the Politician-Magician to recognize you before you get to Prince S.

You write:

(FILL IN THE BLANKS)

Right now, I'm wearing _____*evening wear. It's*
ADJECTIVE

so formal, I could be mistaken for _____
NAME OF FAMOUS PERSON

receiving an award for best _____*. The cloth is*
NOUN

made of the finest _____*. It's* _____ *and*
NOUN   COLOR

covered with _____*, which makes it look*
PLURAL NOUN

_____ *. It looks like it costs* _____
ADJECTIVE   NUMBER

dollars and was made by the _____ *hands of a*
ADJECTIVE

skilled _____. When I _____ in it,
          NOUN   VERB

I look like the fanciest _____ in all of
                                     NOUN

_____. I also have a mask that
NAME OF A PLACE

_____ my face, so no _____ can
VERB ENDING IN "S"   NOUN

_____ me. When anyone sees me in my outfit,
   VERB

they think _____, that's a(n) _____
           EXCLAMATION   ADJECTIVE

_____! My outfit looks like this:
   NOUN

(DRAW YOUR OUTFIT ABOVE)

Your fancy new threads materialize on your body. You admire the workmanship as you inspect your evening wear. A small, rhythmic tapping comes from the desk. You look down and see Phobia has emerged from her drawer. A miniature black velvet cape adorns her thorax, and a tiny tiara glints from between her antennae.

"Wow," she says. "You clean up nice. Love the mask." She scuttles closer to you, and you realize the tapping sound comes from her multiple little high heels. "Whaddaya think? The lipstick's too much, isn't it?" You didn't even know cockroaches had lips.

"You look great," you say.

"I'm gonna hire us a limo," Phobia says. "A stretch limo. I got an enemy who owes me a favor."

CHAPTER TEN

(One Hour Left)

After wading through the flood of filthy lucre and wriggling up and out of an even filthier sewer grate, you find yourself standing in the middle of a freaky, frantic street. Menacing throttles of engines startle you. Blazing red headlights[65] rush toward you over the dingy cobblestones. You scramble onto the sidewalk just as the swarm of driverless motorcycles prowls past.

"Hey, I'm walking here!" Phobia shouts at them. "Lousy motorcycle gangs."

The sudden sound of shattering glass behind you gives

---

65 Headlights function as a vehicle's eyes and so, like all eyes on the Other Side, are red. This only adds to the chaos on the roads, as it's nighttime and, with both headlights and taillights being red, no one knows who's coming or going.

you a terrible jolt. A rabid-looking werehog shoves a shopping cart overflowing with electronics and jewelry through the broken storefront window of a shop called Sketchy Steve's Stolen Goods.

"Now that's what I like to see," Phobia says. "Looting. Sign of a good neighborhood."

Trying to steady your nerves, you take a deep breath of

the thickly polluted air and scan your surroundings. Possessed vehicles drive every which way with no regard for lanes, traffic signals, or even general direction. Bustling shops and dead trees line the grimy sidewalks. Store names pulse in green neon lights: T.J. HEXX, COFFINS 4 U, and BLOODBATH AND BEYOND. Throngs of monsters course in and out of them like blood shuttling through veins.

"Ladyfingers!" bellows a six-foot-tall hot dog standing behind a cart[66] across the street. "Getcha ladyfingers here!" You squint to see what he's selling. The glint of a diamond ring makes you realize it isn't finger-shaped sponge cakes, but actual ladies' fingers. You remind yourself that everything here is fictional, as horrible as it may seem.

"You look like a tourist!" Phobia notices you gawking. "Don't tell me you never been to Hell's Kitchen before!"

"Uh . . . ," you say.

"Whaddaya live under a rock?" she asks. "And if so, what's the rent? It's hard to find decent rocks these days."

Before you can even stammer out a response, Phobia takes off down the sidewalk, completely fearless in the face of the oncoming foot traffic. To follow her, you have to weave your way around a bunch of rotten tomatoes and slide between two boogeywomen.[67] She pauses at the window of Harry's Headless Haircuts.

"Oh! Doesn't she look awful?" she says. Inside, a skeleton in a moldy dress sits in the salon chair. A headless barber wields scissors wildly about in the air several feet away from her. Only a few threads of hair cling to her decaying scalp. "I'm so jealous." Phobia sighs.

---

66 Hot dog vendor

67 Female boogeypersons don't like being referred to as boogeymen. They may be monsters, but they are still ladies.

"Do you think we have time for me to go in?"

"No," you say, "we have to find Prince S."

"All right, all right," she says. "Let's go get our ride. C'mon."

The cockroach darts down an alleyway, and you stay as close on her high heels as you can without crushing her. She rounds the corner and stops under a flickering neon sign that reads THE CANDY BAR.

"I'll meet you inside," she says. "You'll have to take the other door."

She scuttles into a small opening at the foot of the wall. Beside it gapes the darkened entrance for everyone taller than your ankle. Spooky music pours out into the alleyway, and you hesitate for an instant before entering. *What if she's just leading me into a trap? Anything could be inside. Or what if she's purposefully trying to waste my time so Prince S. becomes evil? I should have held her down and plucked her legs off one by one until she pledged loyalty to me.* To think such a vicious thought makes you shudder. It must have been your red voice rearing its ruthless head again. Concentrating on how ridiculous Baron Terrain looked making a poo angel helps you shake it off. You venture inside.

Shadows bathe the crowded room. The only light comes from the displays of candy mounted on the walls like shrines to sugar.[68] Beyond the moving silhouettes of fur, spikes, and horns, your eyes settle on the bar. Hovering behind it, you see what looks like a tooth the size of a bowling ball. You don't see Phobia. Everyone else in the place seems to see you, though. Your heart trembles as dozens of red eyes turn to you. *Do they recognize me? Can they tell I'm a real human?* Not wanting to attract any more attention standing in the doorway, you mosey past the crowd as casually as you can.

The tooth floats over to you. Cavities riddle her yellowed enamel like bullet holes. You doubt she's ever felt the caress of a toothbrush. "Pick your poison," she rasps in a tired voice. Her breath wafts into your face. It stinks of rot. Good thing she can't see the face you make under the mask. Lucky for her, she doesn't have a nose. "We got chockies, gummies, caramels, or do you go in for the hard stuff?"

---

68 Monsters love candy. In the old days, people used to hand out candy to monsters who showed up at their doors on Halloween. Then some clever kids figured out that they could get candy by dressing up as monsters. The monsters are still pretty sore about kids stealing Halloween from them, which is why they eat children whenever they get the chance.

"Ummm . . . ," you say, trying to wave her reeking breath away from your nose. A wall of candy gleams behind her. Mounds of chocolate, bowls of jelly beans, heaps of gumdrops, and glasses of swizzle sticks adorn the shelves. Not to mention stacks upon stacks of every possible bar of candy. "I'll have one of those." You point to a jar filled with large colorful balls.

"A sugar bomb?" she says. A hush falls over the bar. The monsters stop chewing their candy. Even the eerie music cuts out.

The pressure of the room piles on you. *But it's candy,* you think. *How bad can it really be?* "Yeah," you say, feeling bold. "A sugar bomb."

"You asked for it," warns the tooth. "Give me a minute." She disappears behind the bar.

"There you are!" Phobia's voice rings out behind you. "I've been looking all over." You turn to see the cockroach perched on the shoulder of what looks like a classic horror-movie mummy—arms outstretched, body wrapped in bandages—except for the black chauffeur's cap on his head. "I got us a ride. Imhotep here is delighted to drive us to the big shebang."

The mummy groans as if he were dying from the inside out.

"I hope Sweet Tooth didn't get you too jazzed up on the sweet stuff," Phobia says.

Sweet Tooth returns with a multicolored ball on a silver tray. Sparks crackle at the end of its fuse. "Here's your sugar bomb," she says.

"Whoa," says Phobia. "Gettin' bombed before the Wickeding? You're a real party animal!"

The flame inches its way up the fuse. Knowing what you know about Astorya, you should have realized it would be a literal bomb. What you don't know is what it will do to you if you try to eat it, but you doubt it will be good. And you don't have time to find out.

"I'll take it to go," you say.

"Whatever you want," Sweet Tooth replies. She hawks a loogie on the wick, extinguishing the flame.

"Now that's a professional," Phobia says. "Not every bartender would spit on your food like that." She says it as if spitting on your food were some kind of compliment.[69] "Thanks, sugar. Put it on my tab."

You don't really want to touch the spit-frosted ball, but you don't want to offend Sweet Tooth, either, so you shove it into your vest pocket. "Let's go," you mutter,

---

69 On the Other Side, it is.

fully grossed out. Pushing past the sugar fiends and candy freaks loitering in the bar, you and your creepy companions file out the door.

"How far to the Tower of Wrath?" you ask Phobia.

"We should be there in ten," she says. "Unless old bandage brains here gets us lost. Move it, Imhotep!" The mummy shambles into the alley. You follow as your red thoughts rise. *Why is he walking so slowly?! you think. We don't have time for this. Move! Are those bandages flammable? I bet he'd run if I lit a fire under his—*

BOOP.

The sound of a car unlocking interrupts your mental fury. Its red headlights flash to life and you see that it's a stretch limo. Phobia wasn't kidding.

"Open the door for our guest!" the cockroach barks at the mummy. He groans and shuffles toward the back seat.

"I'll do it!" you say, marching toward the door. If you let him open it for you, you'll be here all night.

"You get comfy!" Phobia calls. "I'll ride up front. Me and Imhotep have a lot to discuss." The mummy lets out another groan.

You settle into the cushy back seat of the limo. Ten minutes. You haven't had ten free minutes since you set foot on the Other Side. Your mind reels with all you must accomplish in less than an hour before you become some depraved, fiendish version of yourself. *But what if I don't turn evil?* you think.

A disturbing thought occurs to you. *What if Prince S. was lying about the red voice? What if it isn't evil? What if it makes you stronger? Makes you fearless? What if he doesn't want me to stay on the Other Side because he knows how powerful I would become? I already have the power to make whatever I want. If I were fearless, I would be unstoppable. And then I'd make him pay for lying to me—*

"No!" you scream.

"You all right back there?" Phobia asks from the front seat.

"Fine," you say. "I'm fine." But you don't feel fine. You're losing control of your mind. Your red voice grows stronger with each passing minute. Trying to derail your evil train of thought, you think of Manteau and the other Couriers. You wish you could see their faces right now.

Then you remember you can. Your device. Pride tugs the corners of your mouth into a smile. *I wrote a pretty awesome thing,* you think. *Too bad no one else appreciated it.* You reach into your vest and pull out your device. The warm glow of its screen brings you back to the carefree days you spent at Castle Doodling. You can hardly believe you were there just this morning. It feels like a lifetime ago. Scrolling through the pictures, you land on a close-up of Manteau. You have to admit, he does look handsome, in a huggable, plush-toy kind of way. If he were here right now, he'd probably be pestering you about memorizing the original Original.

The original Original! You still have to memorize it!

You dig into your vest and pull it out. The heavily tinted windows of the limo don't offer much in the way of light. Good thing you wrote a flashlight feature on your device. You tap the screen and turn it on.

A Story of Astorya. You read the words on the page like you did so many times back at the castle. *A bazillion light-years—what if I can't memorize this and I mess it up?* your thoughts needle you. *I will ruin all of Astorya.* You start over. *A Story of Astorya. A bazillion light-years— wait, how long do I have to remember this for? What if the Couriers don't get me home for years? I already forgot everything I should know about myself. What if I forget all of this, too? Maybe something's wrong with me and I can't memorize it.* You strain your eyes, trying to burn the words into your brain. *A bazillion light-years from Earth, there is a place called ASTORYA—why didn't I memorize this earlier? Why did I waste all that time at Castle Doodling?*

And now I'm wasting more time thinking about how I wasted time. You take a deep breath and start again. **A bazillion light-years from Earth**—*how much time do I have left? Seven minutes? Six?* Your eyes scan over the page. So many details. So many potential disasters. *It's no use. I can't do this.* You slump in defeat.

The light from your device beams up at you. You wish the Couriers had listened to you. There would have been no need for this whole fiasco. You could have just taken a picture of the original Original with your device back at Castle Doodling and it would have been safe for all time. And then you wouldn't have to memorize it. You would always have a copy, and there would be no way you could mess it up when you write it in the future. *Why didn't they listen to me?!* You sigh, wishing everything had gone differently, when suddenly, a realization seizes you. You hold the solution.

No one has to know! I can just take a picture of the original Original now. As long as I hang on to my device, I will always have a copy. The thoughts break feverishly in your mind. *And this way, even if I don't find Prince S. or get to the Scarea or get back to the Sunny Side, or if the Politician-Magician destroys the original Original in a poof of smoke, the story will still be safe. I will save*

Astorya. I can explain it all to the Couriers later. They will understand. They will be so proud of me. It's perfect.

"We're almost there!" Phobia shouts back at you.

You chuckle to yourself. You feel like you definitely took the longcut to the shortcut this time. Smiling, you hold the original Original steady in one hand and your device in the other. After a moment or two of trying to get the focus just right, you take the picture. *CLICK.*

Chapter Eleven

Yelling erupts in the front seat. The limo veers wildly to the right. The wheels wail in protest. The limo jerks back to the left. Brakes screech. Rubber burns. The vehicle collides with something. *CRASH!* Metal crunches. Your device and the original Original fly out of your hands as the collision throws you off your seat and onto the door. *SMACK.* Shaking, you grab the original Original and your device off the floor and stow them back in your vest.

"Everyone okay?" you call out. You know in the back of your mind that fictional characters cannot really be hurt, not by a car accident anyhow, but you ask anyway. The foulness must not have taken you yet. You still care. You hear some muffled noises in response.

Opening the door, you stagger to stand. Once outside, you see that the limo has crashed into another limo. It looks identical to yours. Seems like everyone in Monstropolis wants to arrive at the Wickeding of Prince S. in style. You open the front passenger door, and a very shaken Phobia wobbles out.

"That limo came outta nowhere!" she says. You peer into the open door and see your mummy chauffeur slumped over the wheel, groaning.

"Is he okay?" you ask.

"Oh yeah," she says. "He's always like that. Wonder who's in the other limo. Maybe somebody famous. Or rich. Oooh! I got an idea. Quick, pretend you broke your neck. We'll shake 'em down for some cash!" On the Other Side, every monster is evil in their own way. Phobia's evil stems from greed. You've already made her a billionaire and she's still scheming about how to get just a little bit more.

Ignoring her suggestion, you make your way over to the other vehicle as another cockroach stumbles out of its passenger door.

"I think you broke my neck!" the other cockroach says in a voice that sounds exactly like Phobia's. Huh. Are all cockroaches from New York City? And do cockroaches even have necks? "Hope ya got a good attorney," she says. Then you notice this new cockroach looks equally dolled up for the evening—the same black velvet cape, the same tiara, the same heels, and even the same lipstick.

You peer into the other limo and see another mummy slumped over the wheel. This one also wears a black chauffeur's cap. Maybe it's a family business. Maybe it's the mummy's mummy.

Phobia rounds the front of the limo and sees the other cockroach. "Ugh!" she says. "Don't tell me you're going to the Wickeding."

"I'm going to the Wickeding," the other cockroach says.

"Ya gotta be kidding me!" says Phobia. "What are the chances? Two cockroaches wearing the exact same thing.

Listen, honey. One of us is gonna have to go home and change. I nominate you."

"Whaddaya talkin' about?" says the other cockroach. "Looks better on me."

Phobia and the other cockroach turn their red eyes on you. "Whaddaya think?" Phobia says. "Who wears it better? Me. Right?"

"You both look great," you say, not wanting to judge this cockroach beauty contest. Steam curls up from the hoods of the limos. You size up the wreckage and decide that neither of these sweet rides will be going anywhere anytime soon.

As the two cockroaches continue arguing with each other about who looks better, you notice that your body feels stiff and strange. Your evening attire, which fit you perfectly before the accident, now feels tight, as if you gained ten pounds in the last five minutes. Maybe your body has swollen up from shock. But that doesn't sound like something that happens to people from accidents. Broken bones and cuts, yes. Sudden full-body puffiness, not so much.

Not wanting to invite the cockroaches to examine you, which would likely involve them crawling all over your skin, you decide to give yourself a quick pat down. Nothing hurts. Nothing seems broken. You just feel

bulkier, somehow. You remove your mask to get a better look at yourself. But it doesn't help. It feels like you still have the mask on your face, even though you can see that it's in your hand. You touch your face and discover that you had another mask on beneath the mask you were wearing.

Taking off the second mask, you half expect to find yet another underneath it. But this time there are no more masks, just your face. You decide to stash one of them in your vest. When you reach for it, you discover that you have somehow gained another vest lining the first. Two masks. Two vests. What is going on? Next to the S. Word gallantly slung at your waist, you see another S. Word, gallantly slung right next to it. You pull at your clothes and peek underneath, revealing an identical set of your fabulous evening wear.

A feeling of dread squirms up your spine. *Am I hallucinating?* You rip off your outer layers of clothing and hurl them onto the filthy street. It feels real enough. Can you hallucinate a touch? Your mind strains for some explanation. *Maybe I've been here too long,* you think. *Maybe my red voice has taken over and made me crazy!* As you panic, your breath comes fast and shallow. Phobia scuttles over to you. Or at least you think it's Phobia. It might be the other one.

"Hey," she says. "Relax. Ya don't wanna blow all your heavy breathing before we get to the Scarea, do ya?"

The other cockroach taps her heels on the black pavement. "C'mon," she says. "I don't want to miss the Wickeding!"

"You're gonna miss it if ya don't go home and change," Phobia says.

"No can do," she replies. "How 'bout the last one there has to change?"

"Fine with me," Phobia says. "On your mark, get—"

Both cockroaches take off long before the word *go*. What cheats. They rocket away down the grimy sidewalk, their tiny velvet capes billowing as their collective eight heels drum a hasty beat. Steeling your nerves, you push on after the cockroaches with your twin S. Words swinging at your side. Ruined mind or not, you still have to rescue Prince S. Maybe your brain will return to normal if you can get back to the right side of Astorya.

Rounding the corner, you sidestep several saggy-fleshed ghosts spilling out of a doorway.[70] You hustle to keep up with the cockroaches, who move like lightning. But unlike lightning, they're nearly impossible to see.

---

70 This must be a flabby ghast station.

You follow them through an intersection and come to a line of monsters stretching all the way to the end of the block. Two by two, the monsters stand, all dressed in their formal finery. Each one seems to have brought a date to the party. A date that looks exactly like themselves. Perhaps that old adage "opposites attract" doesn't apply on the Other Side. Two vampires, two ghosts, two goblins, two one-eyed purple-feathered sharkbears. But none of them seem happy with dating their mirror image. In fact, they all seem moments away from coming to blows.

When you reach the back of the line, you almost step on your cockroach companions.

"I definitely won," says Phobia. "Ya gotta go change."

"No," the other cockroach says. "I won. You change."

Their argument continues on in an endless loop. You don't have time for this. You head to the front, right past all the monsters bickering and growling at each other. Not one of them notices you skipping the line.

Two massive minotaur security guards wrestle violently behind the red velvet rope. They grapple with each other, their muscles rippling. Horrible steam blasts from their gaping bull nostrils. Equally matched, neither gives any ground. They both rear back and try to headbutt the other, but only succeed in locking horns. As they attempt to disengage their horns with violent jerks of their heads, you seize your chance and squeeze past them through the door.

You steal into a vast, shadowy lobby. Obsidian[71] columns stretch up into a swirling cloud of smoke above your head. The whole place reeks of the Politician-Magician's oily secretions. At the far end of the lobby, an elevator beckons. You slink toward it. From the corner of your eye, a movement makes you jump. You turn to see an exact duplicate of yourself staring back at you.

Oh no, you think. *It's happening to me, too.* You wave at your twin. It waves at you simultaneously. You can't say who waved first. You must have both had the idea at the same time. You inch closer to it. It does the same. *It's a trick!* you think. *This thing isn't a copy of me. It's a monster wearing the same disguise!*

Your fingers wrap around the hilt of one of your S. Words and so do the fingers of your impostor. With your other hand, you rip the mask off your face. Underneath the other's mask, you see your own bewildered face staring back at you.

Then you realize that your identical adversary isn't a copy of you, it's a mirror.

Relieved, you inspect your reflection. Considering

---

71 Dark, glass-like volcanic rock, the perfect building material for classy villains

you've braved a gladiator match, a molten lava maze, and a car crash in the last few hours, you look pretty good. Except for your eyes. You lean closer. You had feared your eyes would have turned almost completely red by now, but it looks like they're only half-full of "the foulness." That might mean you have a little more time, but Prince S. said his transformation could be faster. You secure your mask and hurry into the elevator at the end of the lobby. Instead of doors closing, a thick haze of murky smoke envelops you.

When the smoke clears, you find yourself in an expansive glittering ballroom—if you can call it a room. It doesn't seem to have any walls or a ceiling. A floating chandelier made of crystal bones and diamond skulls refracts the moonlight upon innumerable monster partygoers. All dressed to kill. You feel grateful you wrote yourself such fancy evening wear, especially your mask.

Everywhere you look—the floor, the balconies, the tabletops, the bar, the buffet, the line for the bathroom—you see double. Double dragons, double demons, double trouble. To your relief, no one seems to notice your entrance. They're too busy dancing. Although it doesn't look like any dance you've ever seen. They wallop and thrash and throw each other around. Maybe this is how monsters dance.

On second thought, they're not dancing. They're fighting. Just like the minotaurs at the entrance, the monsters go at their identical counterparts' throats (especially the vampires). You can't hear any music over the din of warring monsters. Looking over to the DJ booth, you see why. Two identical DJs battle, hurling records at each other instead of playing them. The discs slice through the air over the dance floor. One lodges in the neck of a cyclops in a tux. He doesn't seem to notice. He's too busy grappling with another cyclops. Looks like they don't see eye to eye.

You'll never find Prince S. in this mayhem. And you only have precious few minutes before the Wickeding. *I'm too late,* you think. *Just leave him. He'll be fine. Besides, what has he ever done for me?* You clamp your eyes shut and try to lift your own thoughts over the red voice. *So what if he's never done anything for me? So what if he always manages to get himself captured? So what if his memory loss makes it almost impossible to get anything done? He's my friend. What did Manteau say when we escaped the Dust Bunnies? Friends don't let friends get dragged to the Land under the Couch. This whole place is worse than the Land under the Couch. I have to find him.*

He must be here somewhere, he's the guest of honor. You scour the ballroom.

There! You finally spot Prince S.! You dodge and weave through the fray of lashing tails, clobbering fists, punishing claws, and lethal teeth. As you draw nearer to your friend, you see that his face wears that slightly pained expression he so commonly makes when hunting down a forgotten word in the tangled forest of his brain.

"Prince S.!" you call, grabbing his arm.

He jolts out of his brain daze and looks at you. "Have we met before, perchance?" he asks.

You lift your mask for only a heartbeat. "It's me!" you shout over the tumult. "We've got to get out of here!"

"Ah!" Prince S. smiles and replies in your ear, "How fortunate! You arrived just in time. They decided to throw me a party." He takes a look at your fabulous evening wear. "Nice raiment," he says.

The light from the bone-and-skull chandelier dances across Prince S.'s face, illuminating his eyes for a moment. Your heart seizes. Just as you feared, the redness closes in on his eyes. Only a small ring of white remains around each iris. You don't have much time.

"We have to go!" you scream. "We have to hide the original Original and get back home!"

Realization dawns in his reddened eyes. "That's it!" he shouts, elated. "That's what I've been trying to remember. I knew I had something important to do." He notices the extra S. Word hanging at your side. "Another S. Word? What a wonder! I thought there was only one."

Relieved that he can see it, too, you unfasten one of your swords and hand it to him. "Here," you holler.

He grins. "Shall we fight our way out?"

"No, we don't have time. But how do we get you out of here without anyone noticing?"

"'Tis a pity to endure such fame," he says.

If only he had a disguise of some sort. Wait! Remembering the duplicate mask, you dig it out and hand it to him. "Put this on."

Prince S. straps the mask onto his face. You grab his hand and pull him through the monster melee toward the elevator door. You dodge a pair of pommel horses pummeling each other. The rotting hands of zombies graze you. Sizzling pairs of fire skeletons spark and lob flames right past you. Warring twin Hildebeasts[72] go berserk and frenzy at each other, whipping battle-axes about. As you dodge, duck, and dart through the deadly obstacle course,

---

72 Sasquatches wearing lederhosen

a table sails over your head and crashes a few feet from you.

Almost there. You skirt past the overturned table for the elevator. In a poof of smoke, the Politician-Magician materializes in front of you, blocking your path.

Chapter Twelve

(Less Than an Hour Left)

"It'll take more than a couple of masks to fool me." The Politician-Magician smiles, baring his glistening teeth. "I see through all illusions. Lies are my bread and oil." You feel your heart drop clear through the floor, down past the pavement, and into the lava-filled sewer system. Your shining future vanishes. You will never get out of this Tower of Wrath. You will never make it back to the Sunny Side. You will never see your home again. You will never see your friends or family or find out who you really are. Your life will be spent serving this disgusting, oily monster.

"Now, where do you think you're going with my guest of honor?"

Another poof of smoke erupts in front of you. An exact

twin of the Politician-Magician emerges from it. "I think you mean *our* guest of honor," says the twin.

Hope kindles in your heart that these two will start fighting each other like the other monsters. But the Politician-Magician just purrs, "Of course. It's so nice to finally have someone worthy in my presence." So much for the Politician-Magicians fighting each other. He was fond of himself to begin with; now there's twice as much to love.

Prince S. rips his sword from its scabbard. "Out of our way, you pinguid prestidigitators,[73] or face the wrath of my S. Word!"

"You're in no position to make threats," the Politician-Magician says, chuckling.

"Or to talk about wrath," adds the other. "May we remind you that you're standing in *our* Tower of Wrath?"

They cup their hands together. A yellowish globe of oil congeals above their palms and begins to smoke. It reminds you of one of Ember's fireballs. *Uh-oh.*

You reach into your vest for your pencil, but your hand finds something hard and round instead. The sugar bomb from the Candy Bar! You have no idea if it will work as a weapon, but it's your best bet. Just as the Politician-

---

73 A highfalutin way of saying "oily magicians." Prince S. has quite a way with words (when he can remember them).

Magicians' oil ball bursts into green flame, you grab Prince S. by the arm and shout, "Hit the deck!" You hurl the sugar bomb into the fireball and dive behind the table.

BOOM!!! The earsplitting candy blast pushes the table back, bashing into you and Prince S. It doesn't feel good, but it protects you both from the explosion. You peek over the table and see the Politician-Magicians lying splayed out on the floor.

"Now!" you yell, grabbing Prince S.'s hand. The two of you scramble over their unconscious bodies and duck into the elevator. The door of smoke closes like curtains on the chaos roiling over the ballroom.

"I think I found a place to hide the story," you tell Prince S.

"Or we could just stay here," he says, the red in his eyes flashing at you. In that instant, he looks not like Prince S., but some eerie stranger. You recoil from him. Perhaps Prince S. also has a double and you rescued the wrong one. Or maybe his red voice has taken over.

"Don't listen to your red voice, Prince S.!" you say. "Stay with me."

His eyes clench shut as he shakes his head. When he opens them, you recognize him again. The smoke dissipates and the darkened lobby appears before you. You race down the obsidian floor and slip past the minotaur guards (they still haven't managed to loosen their locked horns).

As you lead Prince S. past the line of battling monsters, he says, "The enchantment affects them, too."

"Did the Politician-Magician do this?" you say. "Is he the reason there's two of everything?"

"Perchance he employed his sorcery to make division of them all so that he might appear more popular."

Typical egomaniac. If the Politician-Magician doubled the population, not only would twice as many monsters show up at his party, even more would wish they had been invited.

You scan the line—which at this point has devolved into a full-on brawl—for Phobia and her twin. Looking for a pair of cockroaches in the midst of a monster civil war isn't the easiest task. With all the stamping and stomping, you fear they may have been trampled, which would dash your hopes of ever reaching the Scarea.

"Look what ya did to my tiara!" Phobia's distinctive New York City accent broadcasts her location.

"Well, *you* ruined my cape!" cries a voice just like hers. You follow the sound of the clashing cockroaches. A trail of teensy broken high heels leads you to the Fearmonger showdown. You find them circling each other, dangerously close to the scuffling feet of some ogres. The roaches seem so wrapped up in their own skirmish that they don't notice the ogres could crush them at any moment.

Unable to tell the real Phobia from her double, you fight off your revulsion and grab both cockroaches with your bare hands. Their little legs tickle the insides of your palms. One ogre smashes the other into the wall beside you. You lunge into a less perilous alleyway. Prince S. follows.

"What's the big idea?!" the Fearmongers cry from between your fingers.

"We have to get to the Scarea." You open your palms and bring them to your face. "We have to go right now. What's the fastest way?"

"But we haven't seen the Wickeding yet," they whine in unison.

"It's over," you say. "Prince S. is here."

"Prince S.?" the cockroaches mock you. You can't tell which one says what. "Yeah, right!" "You're full of it!" "What a bunch of phony-baloney!"

Prince S. steps forward. "Ladies," he says, raising his mask so they can get a good look at him. "'Tis my honor to lay mine eyes upon you both."

As far as you know, real cockroaches can't blush, but these fictional ones turn crimson under Prince S.'s gaze.

Dizzy with delight, they roll around in your hands. You cringe in repugnance.[74]

"Oh!" Phobia swoons. "He's almost as good with words as I am!"

"So princely-ish!" the other Phobia gushes.

"So how do we get to the Scarea?" you say, impatience straining your voice. "We need to get there now!"

"Well," Phobia says, "it's outside the city, so the quickest way would be to fly, but you two don't have wings."

"Maybe we can catch a cab," the other roach offers.

"I don't think so," says Phobia. "Look at the traffic! I've never seen it so bad."

You stick your head out of the alley and look up and down the street. It resembles the arteries of a lifelong bacon enthusiast, clogged and dangerous. The sidewalk doesn't fare any better. With seemingly the entire population at fisticuffs[75] with their duplicates, even standing still in this city could end your life.

I should write us a way to fly out of here, you think. *Who cares if they find out I'm real?* Without wasting another moment, you hand off the roaches to Prince S., take out your pencil, and write:

---

74 Extreme disgust, like what you might experience when a cockroach rolls around in your hand

75 An old-timey way of saying "fistfighting," which sounds more civilized than "punching people"

(FILL IN THE BLANKS)

I have a(n) _____ with _____ wings that
             NOUN   ADJECTIVE

can fly in any direction. I steer it with my _____.
                                      BODY PART

It's small enough to _____ in this alley but big
                          VERB

enough for me and Prince S. to _____ on it. It can
                                  VERB

_____ faster than the _____
    VERB   SUPERLATIVE ADJECTIVE

_____, and it has a safety _____ so no
    ANIMAL   NOUN

one will fall. It's in this alleyway right now. It looks like this:

(DRAW YOUR FLYING RIDE BELOW)

"Hey!" Phobia says, eyeing your latest handiwork. "You're in luck! I bet that'll get ya there."

"Which way do we go?" you ask Phobia.

"Follow me," she says.

"No, follow me!" says the other Fearmonger.

The cockroaches spread open their shells and unfurl their wings. With a whirring buzz, they rise like mini helicopters from Prince S.'s hands and flutter upward. You and Prince S. scramble aboard your winged ride before you lose track of your tiny guides.

"A fine steed!" he says, making himself comfortable.

At your command, it rises straight up out of the alley and trails the flying Fearmongers. You quickly lose sight of them. The generous light of the full moon doesn't offer enough to illuminate two insects weaving through the smog-smothered air. Luckily, the twin Phobias continue bickering loudly. With their New York City accents as your compass, you soar over the chaos of Monstropolis below.

Once you leave the evil green lights of the city behind, the moon exposes a desolate landscape stretching out before you. Apparently, the inhabitants of the Other Side prefer city living. *It's a blank slate,* you think. *I could write myself an entire kingdom here. A good kingdom.*

Something to keep Monstropolis in check. That way, I could make sure the original Original was safe. We shouldn't hide it, we should defend it. You feel woozy, both from the height and the thrill of your thoughts. *If I leave, the monsters might find the story. And even if they don't, what's to stop them from coming to the Sunny Side? I have to stay. No one else has the power to fight them. I'll show them what real power looks like!*

Prince S.'s voice falls upon your ear. "Think on the power you wield," he says. "With your mighty pencil, you could write an entire kingdom." Hearing your thoughts echoed from his lips raises your hackles. You must both be falling under the spell of your red voices.

"Stop!" you scream. "Don't listen to it! Think of the other Couriers! Think of Castle Doodling! Think of the sun! We'd never see it again!"

"The sun . . ." His cold voice warms. "I had forgotten her embrace. Her radiance."

One of the Phobias buzzes over to your face. You almost swat at her, before you remember not to. "Almost there!" she says. "The Scarea's just down there on the left. Ya see it?"

Your eyes pore over the empty landscape and settle on what seems to be a faintly glowing area. "Is it glowing?" you ask her.

"That's the one! Let's land here. I don't wanna get too close."

"Me neither," says the other Phobia. "Gives me butterflies!"

The Fearmongers dive toward the ground and you follow. Your winged ride touches down on the grim soil. You and Prince S. slide off.

"Now," Phobia says, her voice dropping to a low whisper. "Are ya ready to be scared?"

"Yes," you say. After all you've already faced, how bad could it be?

"All right," she says. "Follow me. But I'm warning you, this place is no joke."

"No joke," repeats the other cockroach.

"As we approach the Scarea," she says, "you'll notice the land has a glow about it. It's not the good kinda glow. Not eerie or creepy or radioactive. It's the bad kinda glow. The kind that babies have." She shudders as she says the words. "The kind that fresh-baked cookies have."

"The kind that summer vacations have," says the other Fearmonger.

"Enough!" Phobia snaps. "They get it. Now, I wouldn't advise ya to get too close. I can already feel it working on me."

"I can feel it, too!" cries the other one. "It tickles!"

Taking a few steps closer to the glow ahead, you feel something happening. Something subtle and sweet, as if your heart were softening.

Don't go any closer, you think. *It's a trap!*

"I dare not venture farther," Prince S. says as he halts. "Danger is afoot."

"Ya got that right!" says Phobia. "One more step and you'll start whistling. Ya may even giggle."

"What?" you say, trying to make sense of it all. Your heart tells you to go on, but your head tells you to stop.

"Ya see, anyone who gets too close to the Scarea will start to change," she says.

"Start to have good thoughts," the other Phobia adds gravely. "Good feelings."

Good feelings sounds good. I want to have good feelings!

But I should listen to them. They've kept their word so far. We should get out of here!

But it feels good here.

Of course it feels good! It's the last trick of the Other Side! That's how it gets you to finally turn evil. I shouldn't get any closer to it. Everything good about myself will die.

But I want to feel good again. Maybe I should just get a little closer.

Wait! You try to move, but your body freezes in place. *Don't get any closer! It's a trap!* Prince S. stares wide-eyed at you, his face a paralyzed mask of fear.

Look at what this place is doing to Prince S.! Get away from the Scarea! It's going to kill you!

"Stop it!" you scream at your thoughts.

"I wish I could," says Phobia. "But no one can stop the goodness of this place."

Goodness. That's why the monsters fear the Scarea. The goodness here could change them. Make them less evil. Make them want to return home to the Sunny Side. Beckon them back to the days when they lived with everyone else. The days when they were just bad, like the bandits. And not evil.

How this goodness has come to inhabit this patch of the Other Side, you don't know. All you know is that it resists the evil of this place. Just as you must resist.

No! Don't go any closer! your thoughts plead. *RUN AWAY!*

RUN TOWARD IT!

RUN! RUN! RUN! RUN!!!

Gritting your teeth, you wrench one foot forward toward the Scarea and then the other.

TURN AROUND!!!

You slog past the cockroaches toward the glow. With each step, a little of the bitterness you've felt since you arrived on the Other Side ebbs out of your pores.

"What are ya doing?!" Phobia screams at you. "Stop!"

You exhale and a faint fog of darkness escapes your lips. A familiar feeling trickles into your veins. Joy! You laugh and quicken your pace, feeling a spring[76] in your step.

"Are ya crazy?!" the other Phobia shouts.

You can't help but skip closer to the warm glow.

STOP! GO BACK! your thoughts holler at you. But they sound fainter now, more distant, as if they were calling to you from back where Prince S. and the Fearmongers stand. *That's the red voice.* Your own thoughts come to you loud and clear. You feel relieved that you can tell them apart again.

"It's not my fault if ya don't have enough sense to be scared!" Phobia calls out to you. "So don't think you're getting your money back!"

"Yeah!" the other one chimes in. "That filthy lucre is mine!"

"*Yours?*" Phobia sneers.

"Yeah," the second Phobia replies. "Ya heard me."

---

76 Both the kind that bounces and the kind that blooms

"I don't think so!"

You look back and see the two cockroaches flitting away into the night sky, no doubt racing each other back to their subterranean office to defend their pile of gold. Even if the money has doubled along with everything else, you can bet that each Phobia will claim the entirety as her own.

Prince S. remains planted like a Renaissance-themed scarecrow.

"Prince S.?" you say, jogging back toward him. *Yes! Go back! Be with Prince S. He needs you now.* Your red voice grows louder with each of your steps. But Prince S. doesn't budge an inch, he only hangs his head. "Prince S.?" you cry as you draw nearer. Your heart drums with fear. You grab him by the shoulders. The words tremble off your lips. "Are you okay?"

With his eyes closed, he slowly lifts his head, the moonlight falling upon his ashen face. His eyes snap open, glistening like two bloody pools back at you. You search for some trace of white in them, but find none.

"No!" you scream as you stagger back from him. "Prince S.! Don't give in to it! We're almost there!"

He grins wickedly at you. "The hour has passed," he says. "From this time forth, my thoughts be bloody or be nothing worth."

That does not sound good.

Chapter Thirteen

(No Time Left)

"Think of your friends!" you cry to him as you fumble backward. "Remember Manteau? Alicole? What about Larry? And Nova? And Ember!" Returning to the edge of the glowing place, you feel a comforting warmth spread across your back.

The deranged, evil Prince S. chuckles at you. "Those names leave me empty. I shall think of them no more."

It's too late, you think. *He's a monster now, like everyone else here.*

Wait. He's not like everyone else here. He doesn't have a double. Too bad. He could fight him instead of you.

But the S. Word has a double. That gives you an idea.

"Fine," you say. "I'll just take the *real* S. Word and leave."

His red eyes flare. "The *real* S. Word?"

"Yeah," you bluff. "You didn't think I'd give it to you, did you? Yours is a fake."

"Liar!" he roars. "Do you think I know not my own blade?"

"The real Prince S. might," you say. "But he's a lot smarter than you."

He rips the sword from its scabbard. "Impudent rogue! Draw, and let us see if your steel's as sharp as your tongue."

Your hand goes to your hilt, but your mind hesitates. Do you dare raise your weapon? You could never beat Prince S. in a duel. But if you refuse, evil Prince S. might happily slice you to ribbons anyway. You pull the sword from its sheath.

The real Prince S.'s words tumble through your thoughts. *Listen to the S. Word. Don't use it.*

The sword hangs limply in your hand. Maybe yours is the fake. Maybe he holds the real S. Word and yours is a shoddy replica made of aluminum. In that case, it won't be much of a fight.

But maybe yours is the real S. Word and it's trying to tell you something.

"Coward!" Prince S. cuts short your thoughts. "Will you duel?" Your friend may still be in there somewhere, behind the glittering sword and glowering eyes. But you see no shred of him.

Now comes the moment in every superhero's lifetime: the impossible choice. Either scenario leads to your almost certain demise. But what did you expect? You're the protagonist. You have to face these difficult decisions. If it were easy, everyone would do it. But either way, you'd better choose quickly. His flashing eyes tell you that he won't wait any longer.

WHAT DO YOU DO?

If You Fight:

"I will fight you," you say. Your pulse quickens as you move toward him. With each step, you feel the glimmer of goodness within you recede.

Yes, fight him. Your red voice gains strength in your mind. You pause for a moment, unsure if you really should take an action that your red voice supports. It feels dangerous. But so does simply surrendering to the mad captain.

"Then the hour of your death is upon you," he says, his tone so cold it makes you shiver. As if to practice lopping your head off, he fillets the air with his sword. What an invitation.

Calming your nerves, you hoist the S. Word over your head. *Get him!* your red voice growls. With no plan beyond running at him and screaming, you charge at Prince S. He widens his stance as you advance. And when you come

IF YOU REFUSE TO FIGHT:

"I will not fight you," you say. Even if he has lost his mind, he's still your friend. You let your sword drop to the wretched earth. It falls with a dull clang.

"Then you have breathed your last!" Prince S. shouts. He charges you, with the sharp end of his S. Word leading the way, as if he intends to skewer you. When you met this poofy-pants-wearing fellow in Rulette's dungeon and he fell over his own words, gushing out his gratitude at you, you never thought he'd be the cause of your demise. You close your eyes to spare yourself the extra pain of seeing your friend's face twisted with madness.

Prince S. yells wildly as he reaches you. You brace yourself for impact. Many noises follow: a swish, a small thud, the scuffling of feet, and then a much heavier thud.

You unclench your eyes to see Prince S. out cold on the ground. The S. Word lies beside him.

upon him, you throw the S. Word down on him as hard as you can.

CLANG!

The sound of the swords meeting rings through your skull. In a flash of silver, Prince S. strikes your S. Word out of your hand and it falls to the dirt. He spins around you and knocks your knees out from under you, making you crumple to the ground. He rips off your mask and slashes a cursive *P* and *S* onto your face, stinging each cheek with a letter.

"Eat my leek!" he proclaims, standing over you, the tip of his sword lingering at your throat. "I shall wait till your eyes match your cheeks. Then you shall fully inhabit your wrongful mind."

Just give in, your red voice murmurs in your head. *You won't feel any more pain soon.* If the red voice dealt in honesty rather than deceit, it would have also told you that soon you wouldn't feel love anymore. Nor would you ever feel peace again. Your ability to hope would evaporate. Friendship would no longer hold any meaning for you. And all forms of happiness—from joy to satisfaction and from pleasure to fun—would forever remain out of your reach. Once the redness blots out the whites of your eyes, only hatred thrives in your heart.

You can't imagine what kind of critical fail just happened to Prince S. You wish that you had seen it. Just like how it wouldn't allow you to strike the legs of the Big Rock Candy Mountain Man, the S. Word, in its wisdom, must have made Prince S. miss. Not only miss, but knock himself senseless. You don't know how long evil Prince S. will remain unconscious. His red eyes might flutter open at any moment. As a precaution, you grab his S. Word (as well as your own) and secure them to your belt. Looking down at his peaceful, sleeping face, you wonder if the redness may loosen its grip on him if you can get him farther into the Scarea. Seizing your chance, you drag Prince S. by his buckled shoes.

As you heave him toward the glowing terrain, you wish you had gone to the Other Side with one of the smaller Couriers, like Manteau or Ember. Then you think of Larry and Alicole, and realize your load could be much heavier. But just thinking of your friends, heavy and light alike, cheers you.

He needs help! your red voice cries as you watch a bump the size of an egg swell up on his head. *Take him back to Monstropolis!* As if any monster there would even consider helping you. The foulness must be getting desperate. Your red voice sounds far away now, like a little kitten mewling

A hatred that consumes you.

At first, you focus your hatred on Monstropolis and the hideous monsters who live there. Like Rulette, you write yourself your own army. But unlike Rulette, you win. Your army levels Monstropolis and enslaves the monsters there. To your great displeasure, rather than relieving your hatred, your victory only makes your hatred grow. You write yourself and Prince S. a kingdom: Angerdom. But you loathe every stone of it.

Your hatred turns to the Sunny Side and the other Couriers. You prepare for war with them, and when they come one day, looking to rescue you, you capture them and trap them until they, too, see red. But you hate the evil Couriers even more. Most of all, you hate Prince S. You hate the scars he left on your face. *P.S.* Like you, yourself, are some kind of afterthought. A postscript. A joke. Your hatred demands that you banish him and the others to a realm far from Angerdom.

But you know that because of the way Astorya works, they still exist. And you hate that they exist. You hate that all of Astorya exists. And one day, you decide the only way to quench your hatred is to erase Astorya in its entirety.

And in this, you are correct.

On day 4,692 of your evil reign, you erase the original

from outside your window. You almost feel sorry for it. Almost.

As you lug the unconscious captain, you notice the strange, comforting glow of the Scarea, as well as your own glowing feelings, grows stronger. You finally come to a small crack in the earth. The glow emanates from somewhere inside the crevice. You let go of your friend's limp legs and take in a deep breath of fresh air. Air! Not that stuff that passes for air on the Other Side, but real, honest-to-goodness Astoryan oxygen. Standing there, breathing heavily like you just won a hundred-yard dash, you feel so happy you could frolic.

But then you remember you have a mission: hide the original Original.

You consider your surroundings. Even if the monsters fear this place, it feels wrong to just leave the story sitting in this little hole in the ground. You reach down into the crack, but feel nothing, not even the bottom of the hole. For a moment, your heart freezes in terror. What if this is one of the Three Holes? And when you pull your arm back out, you have nothing but a stump where your hand should be? Preparing for the worst, you bring your hand back up.

To your infinite relief, you find it still attached to your arm.

Original. And, finally, you are free from your hatred. The curse of the Other Side that reddened your eyes lifts just as the very land you stand on and the air you breathe vanishes. Only space surrounds you. As you float, holding your very last breath, it all comes back to you like a flood. You feel all the love, all the hope, all the joy, all the friendship you have been missing, followed by a regret as vast as the cosmos in which you float. Because you gave in to your red voice, you never got to see your home again. Never got to see your friends. Or your family. You never got to find out who you really are. Instead, you became a thing of hatred. A destroyer of everything, including yourself. You can't stop your tears, and without gravity, they drift out of your eyes and form perfect spheres that orbit your face like tiny glass moons. You feel like you've never seen anything so beautiful.

You want to laugh from the joy of feeling beauty again, but you don't want to let your breath out. Not yet. Not when your life is finally worth living again. You wish you could make these last seconds last an eternity. But they slip away from you, just like the air in your lungs.

THE END

Feeling a little more confident, you peek into the crevice. The light inside dazzles you. You squeeze your eyes shut and let the blinding rays bathe your face. They feel wonderful on your skin. Your whole body tingles with warmth, even though only your head pokes through the hole.

I know this feeling . . . it's sunlight!

Could the sun be spilling in from the Sunny Side? Did you just stick your head into some kind of subterranean shortcut back?

Your heart throbbing with excitement, you scramble over to your sleeping friend and drag him to the hole. It looks like a tight fit, especially with those big poofy pants of his, but you think you can squeeze him in.

You lower your legs into the crevice, searching for something to stand on. But like the inside of the GPS, this place follows its own rules of gravity. What ought to be down turns out to be sideways. You swing your legs around and find some kind of ledge. It feels sturdy enough, once you get over the weirdness of your body being parallel to the ground.

Grabbing Prince S., you try to pull him in with you. You have to wrestle and jerk your friend's unconscious body this way and that. Amazingly, he doesn't wake up. The S.

Word really must have done a number on him. You hope his head injury doesn't make his memory even worse.

At last, he tumbles in with you, bringing a cascade of soil and pebbles with him. Some of the dirt falls off the ledge and spills down into an abyss below you.

You reel back from the edge.

As your eyes adjust, you see that the light streams out of

the wall across an enormous expanse. Perhaps through a crevice like the one you just entered. What appears to be sidewalks extend over the forbidding chasm. Some reach upward, some downward, others diagonally, but most stretch out level over the yawning pit like narrow bridges made of white squares.

Familiar shapes on some of the sidewalk squares catch

your attention. Letters! Large capital letters. Suddenly, the place looks like a three-dimensional crossword puzzle that someone gave up on partway through: Most of the squares are blank. But the ledge you stand on has a word on it: *DANGER*. Seems fitting, as this ledge is hardly wide enough for you and your unconscious companion. If he were to roll over in his sleep, he would fall into the infinity below. Let's hope he sleeps like a log.[77]

Not taking any chances, you test the blank tile leading from the *D* in *DANGER* with your toe. Your foot passes right through it. Gasping, you stumble backward. Your heart pummels the inside of your chest. That could have been your last step. But the tile looked solid. The only difference between it and the square you stand on is that yours has a letter on it.

What did Prince S. say before you leapt into the Galick Sea? Something about how letters make words, words make stories, and stories make the world. Perhaps the crack you entered is a tear in the fabric of Astorya and these letters are like the letters you saw in the Galick Sea, more building blocks of this fictional reality.

---

77 A stationary log, not one of the rolling variety

A plan brews in your mind as you survey the crossworld crossing before you. Maybe if you write a letter on the blank tile, it will become solid and support your weight. And if so, you can keep coming up with words and navigate across the void. It won't be easy, though. With no guardrails of any sort, these sidewalks provide little safety. It will only take one slip, trip, or wobble to send you hurtling off into oblivion.

Four blank spaces extend out before you. So you need a five-letter word starting with *D*. You glance back at Prince S. You could really use his help right about now. But his great collection of words remains locked behind his inert lips. He just peacefully sleeps on the word *DANGER*.

You may not have access to Prince S.'s words, but you do have access to a whole book of words. And it just so happens that the words you need to solve the puzzle all appear in this very book. For clues, turn to page 332.

Steadying your nerves, you inch up to the edge. With the tip of your pencil leading the way, you reach out into the blank tile and trace out a letter in the space. As soon as you finish, you feel a remarkable sensation underneath your pencil: resistance.

Tapping it with your fingers just to make sure, you find the square now feels solid to the touch. You test it with your foot. It feels every bit as strong as the one you stand on. Slowly, you shift your weight onto it. Rather than plunging into the abyss, you remain secure on your newly written letter. It worked! Now you just have to solve the rest of the words, haul the sleeping Prince S. in tow, and try your best to not fall to your death.

(CONNECT THE LETTERS TO FORM WORD BRIDGES TO GET TO THE OTHER SIDE. GO TO PAGE 332 FOR THE CLUES.)

At last, you write the final letter connecting you to the ledge just below the light. You feel hopeful as you read the word *SAFETY* written on it.

After dragging Prince S. to *SAFETY*, you take a closer look at the break in the wall, just above the *T*. You peek through and your heart swells like a hot-air balloon. Green grass, blue sky, a late-afternoon sun. Have you made it back to the Sunny Side?

Every fiber of your being wants to crawl through that hole. But then you remember the mission. You'll have to leave the original Original here. This strange space in between the two sides of Astorya seems like a pretty safe hiding spot.

You dig into your vest and pull out the story. The page looks tattered and worn, not to mention filthy from the time it spent in the Land under the Couch. You hold it up to the light streaming through the crack in the wall and see a tiny pinprick of a hole in the paper. A tear in the page. Astorya being such a literal place, you don't doubt that the tear on the story could very well be the same tear that created this crossworld chasm.

Just in case someone (or something) comes wandering into this strange space, you decide you should take the original Original back to the middle of the puzzle.

That way, you can erase the words before and after it, preventing anyone fictional—or any real person without a real-world pencil—from reaching it.

You set out, walking back carefully along your word bridges, and arrive at what you believe to be the middle, mostly because you found the word *MIDDLE* there. Cautiously, you get down onto your hands and knees and shuffle along backward, erasing each letter of the connecting word closest to the Other Side as you go. Once back on the middle, you smooth out the precious page and lay it down in the middle of the word *MIDDLE*.

It doesn't feel right to just leave it here like that. This place doesn't seem to have any weather, but what if somehow a storm blew through here? Or even if a gentle breeze puffed through one of the tears, the page could slide off and drift down into the darkness. You should write something to secure it. The whole world of Astorya relies on this one piece of paper. It deserves a royal receptacle.

You grab your pencil, dreaming up something truly magnificent to protect the original Original. You write:

(FILL IN THE BLANKS)

The _____ **Box**
ADJECTIVE

There is a box in front of me right now. It's _____
COLOR

and covered in _____. *It looks so* _____
PLURAL NOUN   ADJECTIVE

that a(n) _____ *would be afraid to even* _____
NOUN   VERB

near it. It's indestructible, so no one can _____ *it.*
VERB

Even the _____ _____ *in the*
SUPERLATIVE ADJECTIVE   NOUN

universe can't hurt it.

Just as you wrote it, the box appears in front of you.
You admire your handiwork. It looks formidable, just as
you described it. But though it's indestructible, some
unforeseen adversary might still manage to open the box
and get at the precious treasure inside. So just to be safe,
you add:

Only I or one of the Couriers can open the box.

You place *A Story of Astorya* into your indestructible
box. Then you remember what the Couriers said about
you writing something to protect the original Original. The
problem with using a fictional object to hide a real piece
of paper is that the fictional object is only as safe as the
paper it's written on. You would have to write a story to
protect the story protecting the original Original. And you
would have to keep writing stories to protect the stories
protecting those stories. You hear Ember's voice in your
head: *infinite fortresses.*

As you sigh in frustration, a brilliant idea percolates in

your mind. *What if I just put the original story of the box inside the box?*

Now you're thinking. No one but yourself or one of the Couriers would ever be able to get to it. So with its Original safely sealed inside it, your box would truly be indestructible. You don't have to write infinite invincible boxes, you just have to put the story of the box *inside the box.*

You place the freshly written story of the box inside the box next to the original Original. A wide grin spreads out on your face as you close the lid of your magnificent container. *CLICK.*

You crouch down and begin erasing the path to the word *MIDDLE,* all the while marveling at your own cleverness and basking in the thrill of victory. Before you finish, you hear a groan behind you. Prince S.! Looking back, you see him stir from where you shoved him up against the wall.

As quickly as you dare, you make your way over the narrow word bridges to your friend. Your hand goes to the hilt of one of your S. Words, just in case the foulness of the Other Side still lingers in him. He moans softly, making a sound somewhere between a yawn and a whimper. Deciding that even evil Prince S. wouldn't stand a chance against you in his current state, you kneel down and help him to his feet.

With your friend leaning on your shoulder, you push your head through the crack in the wall. He lets out another moan and some garbled words that sound like "My bloody pate," whatever that means. You'd better get him out of here before he comes to and sees where you hid the story. You squeeze through the tear in the wall and lug your semiconscious friend through after you.

CHAPTER FOURTEEN

*T*he sun casts its balmy rays through the leaves of gently swaying trees. The air feels warm and calm, like four o'clock on a clear day in spring. The despair and rage that clouded your mind on the Other Side have fully dissolved.

Lying on his back, Prince S. flickers open his eyelids. "Where am I?" he murmurs. "Fair daylight?" Not a trace of red remains in the whites of his eyes. You laugh in relief, and then take a deep breath of the luscious air and laugh again, elated at how good it feels to breathe clean oxygen. Prince S., making a seemingly instantaneous recovery, leaps to his feet and says, "Dear Heavens! The original Original! Is it safe?"

"It's safe," you say. It would have been nice if he had

shown such vitality when you were working your way through the crossworld puzzle. "It's safer than it's ever been, and it'll stay that way forever."

"Say no more, lest I remember too much of its whereabouts." He smiles at you, tapping his head. "Your cunning is sharper than a serpent's tooth!" You grin, slightly disappointed that you can't share with him the most cunning part about how you wrote an indestructible box to keep the story safe. After you hand him one of the S. Words, he fastens it onto his waist and says, "Now then, where are we?"

"I think we're back on the Sunny Side," you say.

Prince S. tugs at his beard and surveys the surroundings. Just beyond the crest of a nearby hill, you can make out what looks like a small city.

"Look!" you say, pointing it out to him.

"Civilization!" Prince S. says.

"Let's go!" you say and sprint off down the hill toward the city with your fictional companion close behind. The air tastes so good, it practically sparkles on your tongue. You feel like you're flying rather than running.

Before long, you and Prince S. find yourselves on a quiet residential road on the outskirts of the city. Cheerful pink and yellow flowers overflow the window boxes. A purple

teddy bear waves at you from a window. You wave back. Another purple teddy bear pops in front of the first and waves more energetically at you. The sight of the second bear makes you gasp.

"Prince S.," you say, "do you see those bears?"

"Indeed!" he says. He doffs his cap at the bears, who jostle each other out of the way, trying to secure the best place at the window to wave at you. "They're falling over themselves to welcome us!"

"But there are two of them," you say.

"Vex not yourself on such a splendid afternoon," he says. "We left the curse of the doubling behind."

Nodding, you tell yourself that many teddy bears look alike.

The thundering of hooves draws your attention from the window. Ahead, you see a shimmering black unicorn gallop around the corner and charge toward you.

"I'm the fastest!" the unicorn huffs as he runs, foam dripping from his mouth.

"Impossible!" brays an identical voice as an identical unicorn rounds the corner. "I am! There can be only one!" The unicorns race down the street, jockeying for the lead. You and Prince S. jump out of the way as they barrel past.

"Galfalador?" Prince S. says as he watches them go.

"The Onyx Unicorn of Splendidia? I didn't know he had a brother."

"He doesn't," you say, your heart sinking. "Don't you see what's happening?"

"Now," Prince S. says weakly, "my memory may be failing me." That seems extremely likely, but you avoid commenting. "Perchance there were two unicorns in that story . . ."

A piercing cry cuts short his recollection. It comes from somewhere up ahead.

"Sounds like someone needs help," you say.

"Perchance a damsel in distress?" he says.

"Let's go!" you say.

"A hero's work is never done!" he says, happy to be of use again.

You both hurry up the city street toward the sound of the crying, which grows louder and more heartbreaking the closer you get to it. When you reach the market square, you see its source. Two men in vests and billowing shirts stand crying in the center of the plaza. Their tears cascade down their cheeks and pool at their feet. If it weren't for the horrible wailing, they'd make a good fountain.

"What troubles you?" Prince S. shouts at them.

"It's awful!" cries one of the men.

"Terrible!" cries the other.

"Unthinkable!" cries the first. "There are two of everything!"

"Two of everything!" cries the other.

"Stop repeating everything I say!" sobs the first. "*I'm* the Town Crier!"

"No, *I'm* the Town Crier!" wails the other, and they both crumple into blubbering heaps on the pavement.

"See what I mean?" you yell to Prince S. over their sobs. Trying to block out the sound of the Town Criers, you take in your surroundings. Doubles. Everywhere you look. Two bananas in bandanas trip over two pairs of two left feet. Two nurse sharks hop over on their tails to help and fall into each other, getting tangled up in their bandages. A couple of trench-coat–clad detectives bang into each other and knock themselves down as they rush over to investigate. A pair of cat burglars slink out of an alley and attempt to pick the detectives' pockets, but end up getting into a catfight.

"Dear Heavens!" exclaims Prince S. "Can it be so? Mine eyes see twice of all they gaze upon! But I know full well the magic of the Politician-Magician cannot reach the Sunny Side."

The spectacle before you strips your words from your tongue. *What happened?* Maybe this isn't the Sunny Side. Maybe that crossworld puzzle led you to a parallel dimension. Or maybe this is the final trick of the Other Side, a place that looks sunny but is actually just as evil. But then you see a familiar sight. In the distance, towering over the buildings and houses, sits the Old Factory.

"Spielburg!" you exclaim. "We're in Spielburg."

"Spielburg?" Prince S. says in astonishment. "But this is not the city I know by that name."

"New Spielburg," you say. "I had to redraw it after Rulette erased the old one."

"But if this is the Sunny Side," he says, "what has brought this plague of copies upon us?"

The word rattles you. *Copies.* The weight of the world dumps upon your shoulders. Is it possible that all of this has something to do with the copy you made of the original Original?

"What if . . . someone . . . made a copy of the original Original?" you ask Prince S. "Would there be two of everyone in Astorya?"

"That would follow, yes," he replies. "But why would anyone do such a thing? And how? I thought you ensured its safety."

"Oh, I did. The original Original's fine," you say. But you don't feel fine. Your stomach sinks like you just swallowed a pound of lead. It's your fault. You did this when you took the picture of the original Original. The car crash. Two limos. Two mummy drivers. Two Phobias. Two of everyone. You made a copy of the story that makes the entire world. And in doing so, you made a copy of the entire world.

"Hold on," you say. You fish your device out of your vest and scroll through the images on it. Manteau making a kissy-face. Larry holding a heart doodle, making himself look less formidable. Alicole holding her crossbow, making herself look more formidable. Nova waving with all four of her arms. Ember scowling. Finally, you land on that fateful picture of the original Original. You search the screen for the delete button, but you can't find one.

Then you remember that you wrote this device to not have a delete button. At the time, it seemed like a good idea. You wanted to be sure anything stored on it couldn't get erased like all the paper Originals. But now you can't undo what you've done. You can't erase the copy of the original Original.

"I think I know what's going on," you say. "It's all because of my device."

"That ill-conceived contraption of yours?" he asks.

"We have to destroy it," you say.

All at once, the creepy feeling of being watched crawls up your spine. Eyes everywhere suddenly lock on you. But not all the eyes. Only half of them. One of every pair of the New Spielburgers stares at you. They must be the copies.

"Do you see that?" you say, keeping your voice down.

"See what?" he says.

"The copies. They're all looking at me."

He surveys the crowd. "So they are," he says. "Perchance they are impressed by your evening wear."

"No," you whisper, "I think the copies can hear us."

"Why shouldn't they?" he says. "Do they not have ears?"

"No, I think they can *all* hear us. Through the device."

"What a curious idea," he says. "Is that why you seek to destroy the device?"

As soon as he says "destroy the device," the stares of the copies sour into menacing glares. Everywhere you look, the doubles, as if moving to the beat of a single drum, step forward toward you and Prince S. Your eyes dart up and down the street for a place to escape, but find only more fuming doubles.

"We'd better get out of here," you say, grabbing Prince S. by the hand and heading back the way you came.

You don't want to venture any deeper into this densely populated city.[78]

"Why?" he asks, oblivious to the hostile copies. "To destroy the device?"

"Stop saying that!" you plead as you yank Prince S. along.

"Saying what? 'Destroy the device'?"

"SHHHHH!!!"

Moving as one, the doubles all take another step toward you and Prince S. The sound of their collective feet (paws, hooves, flippers) hitting the ground together makes your heart trip over its own beat.

"Run!" you yell, breaking into a full sprint. Prince S. scrambles after you as you hightail it back to the outskirts of town.

"GET THEM!!!" cries the duplicate Town Crier in a deafening voice.[79] All at once, like a flock of birds taking wing, the duplicates begin marching toward you from all sides. The open space around you disappears as they close in on you.

"What have we done to incur such wrath?" Prince S. calls out.

---

78 Its population doubled as of today!
79 You can see why he got the job.

"The device!" you say. "It's telling them what we're saying!"

You race back through the streets toward the entrance to the town, feeling the invisible daggers of eyes on you with every breathless step. Doors burst open, and duplicates of every shape and size emerge, joining in the eerie lockstep pursuit. It looks like a bizarre military parade made up of the imagination of all humankind, which would be delightful to witness if they weren't trying to kill you.

You make it to the outskirts of town with the doubles marching close behind. They don't show any signs of giving up the chase. Your hand reaches for your pencil as your heroic sprint slows into a wheezing trot. You doubt you could write a single word before they were upon you, let alone something that would rescue you from this furious multitude.

"Behold!" Prince S. gasps. "Our umber[80] sky chariot awaits!"

Like a glorious brown sunrise, the Giant Poop Ship appears over the crest of the hill. Overwhelming joy revives your weary limbs. You bound up the hill as the ship glides down toward you.

---

80 A natural pigment, usually dark yellowish brown in color and thus an appropriate description

Glancing back, you see that the copies have stopped marching. Maybe they know better than to tangle with the Couriers. They gather at New Spielburg's city limits, watching your great escape.

CHAPTER FIFTEEN

The sphincter opens on the surface of the GPS. The blue light of the poop chute beams down to you and Prince S. Cradling you in its rays, the light lifts you off the ground and up into the safety of the ship. The sphincter closes tight behind you, but your guilt opens wide as you ascend the poop chute, ever closer to having to tell Prince S. and the other Couriers what you did.

The blue light deposits you and Prince S. on the floor.

ZSCHOOM. The sliding door opens, revealing the bright heart of the ship.

Trying not to drag your feet, you step through the door and orient yourself to the gravity inverter. No hero's welcome awaits you. No one even says hi. You look around at your friends. Alicole wears a somber expression. Ember glowers at you from the command center. Larry doesn't even scuttle over to give you one of his spiky insect hugs. Maybe they already know it's your fault.

"A plague of copies runs amok in Astorya!" Prince S. announces.

"We are fully aware," Alicole says.

"Where's Manteau?" you say.

"Dancing." Ember rolls her eyes at you, as if the answer to your question should have been obvious.

"He's dancing to distract the duplicate Couriers," says Larry. "While we try to figure out what to do."

Duplicate Couriers? Oh no. Since Prince S. doesn't seem to have a copy, you had hoped that somehow the Couriers would be spared from the disastrous doubling. No such luck. You want to beg their forgiveness for your rash decision to make a copy of the original Original, but before you have a chance, Prince S. asks, "And what of our brilliant chamalien engineer?"

"She's going head-to-head with the other Nova back at Castle Doodling," Ember says.

"A telepathic battle of wits?" Prince S. muses. "Each one knows the other's mind. I venture neither has even made a first move yet."

"The original Original," Alicole says, turning to you. "Did you succeed in your mission?"

"I did," you say, relieved that she changed the subject. You wish you could share with them what a clever hiding spot you found and tell them all about your crazy adventure on the Other Side. But that would defeat the whole purpose of you going. At least you don't have to police your own thoughts, you think. One benefit of not having Nova on board.

"That's great," Larry says, trying to sound upbeat. "You were able to hide it on the Other Side?"

"Yes," you say. But you can't help but think that you didn't exactly hide it on the Other Side. More like the Inside, or the Place Between Sides. You wonder if the Couriers know that a rip in the actual paper of the original Original tears the landscape and makes a gateway into the very fabric of Astorya itself.

"You sure it's safe?" Ember asks. "Like no one will be able to find it?"

You suppose some New Spielburger could happen upon the tear one day. But unless another Rulette came along with a real-world pencil, he or she or it couldn't complete the word bridge to the box, and even then, if somehow someone got hold of the box, only you or a Courier could open it. "Yeah," you say, feeling confident, "it's safe."

"Tell us no more," Alicole says. "You've told us all we need to know."

But they don't know you made a copy of the original Original.

"It's all my fault," you blurt out, unable to keep it inside. "I did it. I took a picture of the story with my device,

I made a copy of the original Original."

"You did this?" Prince S. cries, his face pained with disbelief. "Whatever for? Did I not warn you of the chaos that would come from meddling with the mechanism of our universe? Why would you do such a foolhardy thing?"

You think back on that moment in the limo. Maybe this isn't your fault. Maybe the red voice made you do it. Everything was so confusing on the Other Side. You were fighting for control of your mind. Mistakes were bound to be made. You feel the weight of the blame lift off your shoulders.

But only for an instant.

Because you know the truth. It wasn't the red voice. It was you.

And it happened before you even got to the Other Side.

You wasted your time. You did everything but what your friends were counting on you to do. You rode the slides. You drank the cocoa. You played with your device. But you didn't memorize the story.

"Because I didn't memorize it," you say. "I was afraid I would mess it up. But now I've messed everything up. I'm sorry. I'm really sorry."

Prince S. shakes his head in dismay and you look away, not wanting to see his exasperation. "But I can fix it, I think. I just have to find the original story of the device."

"How is that going to help?" Ember snipes.

You hesitate. You know how the Couriers feel about erasing stories. But once again, erasure seems like the only solution.

"I have to erase it," you say. The Couriers stiffen and you feel their resistance. But you go on. "The only way to get rid of the copies is to erase the story of the device. We can't delete the picture I took. So we have to erase its Original and destroy the device." No one says a word. Their silence crushes you. You turn to Alicole. She took the story from you. She should know where it is. "Alicole," you say. "Do you remember what you did with the story?"

"It's back at Castle Doodling with the other Originals," she says. "But first, we need you to fix the situation with the duplicate Couriers. Manteau cannot keep dancing for much longer. When we arrive at Castle Doodling, we will need you to write something to imprison them. A trap they can't escape from. Then we can figure out what to do next."

"Okay," you say, but you feel that her plan falls short. "I can write a jail or something for them. But what about all the other copies? You know, when we were in New Spielburg, they could all hear what I was saying. And then they all came after us at the same time. It was really weird."

"That's because that's how you wrote it," Larry says. "The device is connected to all of them. So it shares anything it hears with all the copies instantly. It's a really impressive piece of technology you wrote."

Finally, the appreciation you had hoped for, but it only makes you feel worse.

"But the duplicates paid us no heed on the Other Side," Prince S. says.

"You didn't threaten the device until you came back here," Ember says, "so they had no reason to threaten you."

"So what about all the duplicate Doodlings?" you ask. "Are they all going to attack me?"

"As long as you don't do anything else to threaten the device," says Alicole, "you should be safe enough."

"But if it hears you talking mean about it, we might not be able to protect you," Larry says. "There are a lot of Doodlings."

"So, it's really listening to us? All the time?" you say, wrenching your device out of your vest. "I wrote it to help us, not spy on us!" What an invasion of privacy. Betrayed by your own creation. Those copies could have killed you.

And your device told them to.

"Can you not shut the wretched thing down?" Prince S. asks.

"No, I wrote it so it can't turn off. And because it's fictional, it doesn't matter if I flush it down the toilet or stomp it to pieces. It'll still work!" You feel trapped. Anger boils over inside you. "I hate it! I wish I never wrote it!"

You hurl your device to the floor.[81] It feels good to throw it. You wish you could throw this whole disaster away and be done with it. But, as you knew it would, your device bounces a few times and then settles, totally unharmed.

"Curse that infernal contraption!" Prince S. rages at the device. "How can we feign pleasantries around it while it ruins this very world? Making everyone an enemy of themselves? If it truly listens to every word we utter, hear me now—we will find a way to end this madness!"

After a moment, Larry says gently, "So . . . I think that would count as talking mean to it. Just try not to do that when we get to the castle."

"I don't want it anywhere near me," you say. "Let's just

---

81 Which, in the GPS, is also the wall. And the ceiling.

leave it here. Then it can't listen to me."

"Good thinking," Alicole says. "The device shall stay here. Just don't leave your pencil behind. We will arrive at any moment. Captain, if I may take leave, I should like to fly the perimeter of the castle in case any of the duplicate Couriers have managed to escape."

"A worthy strategy," Prince S. says. "Go with a quickness!" The door opens—*ZSCHOOM*—and Alicole trots out, crossbow in hand. "Now," Prince S. says, "when we infiltrate the castle, remain close in case Manteau has failed to keep the false Couriers entranced." You and the rest of the Couriers gather around Prince S. and follow him through the door. *ZSCHOOM.*

You pass through the front door of the castle unchallenged. When you enter, you push past hundreds of scampering Doodlings. Your party wends and winds through the doodles and their doubles toward the dining hall. "Be careful when we open the door," Ember says. "Manteau's still dancing. So don't look."

"Larry," Prince S. says, "you shall kick open the door and enter backwardly with wings unfurled to block our view of Manteau's dance."

"Okay, Captain," Larry says.

"Maybe I should go in backward, too," you say. "Just in case." You don't want to get mesmerized yourself by secondhand stoat dancing.

"As you wish." Prince S. draws his S. Word from its scabbard. "I shall take up the rear."

"The duplicate Couriers should be on the stage," Ember says to you. "So that's where you should write the trap."

"Got it," you say, taking out your pencil.

"Luck, friends!" Prince S. says.

CHAPTER SIXTEEN

*L*arry kicks open the door and scuttles in. He turns to face you and unfolds his shell segments, nearly doubling his width. Ember runs and flips up onto one of his legs. Your pulse throbbing, you spin around and walk backward through the door. Prince S. steps through the door facing you, ready to fend off any attack.

Aside from the rustling of papers as Larry backs into the piles of Originals, you hear the sound of a small mammal exerting himself. Good old Manteau! He still keeps his audience captive. As Larry plows backward, Originals collect on either side like mini mountain ranges.

You shuffle one foot behind the other, catching glimpses of the stage reflected in the raised blade of Prince S.'s sword. Flashes of the mesmerized faces flicker at you. Baron Terrain, then the other Alicole and the other Larry, Nova, Manteau—

Wait.

Nova. Didn't Ember say that Nova was locked in some kind of brain-off with her duplicate? Then why is she onstage?

Then something horrible occurs to you.

What if that Nova is the real Nova? What if all the Couriers onstage are the real Couriers? What if the *duplicates* picked you up?

You shudder, thinking back to the GPS. They weren't very friendly. They didn't get nearly as upset as you feared they would when you told them how you inadvertently made copies of everyone. And didn't Ember say something weird about you threatening the device? How could she have known that? She wasn't there.

There's only one way she could have known. The device told her. She's not the real Ember. None of them are real. They're all duplicates. And they're trying to trick you into trapping your friends!

Eyes bulging, you stare at Prince S. and mouth the words, *They're copies.*

What? he mouths back at you.

They're copies. You contort your face, trying to silently communicate to Prince S. The expression on his face tells you that you failed. If only he could read your mind.

Uh-oh. He can't read your mind. But someone else can. The duplicate Nova. She could be reading your mind right now.

You look down at the page in your hand. If Nova can hear what you're thinking, you've got to act fast. You can't set the trap around the false Couriers, otherwise you and Prince S. will be imprisoned along with them. But if you can stop Manteau's dance, the real Couriers may come back to their senses in time to protect you from the duplicates, who will no doubt be less than thrilled at your deception.

You drop to your knee and Prince S. stands guard over you. Smoothing the paper out on your thigh, you scribble out:

A(n) _____ *forms around Manteau too small*
          NOUN

for him to _____ *in.*
          VERB

The sound of a small, furry creature smacking into the side of your trap rings out in the dining hall, followed by an "Oof!" Your plan worked!

"The duplicates!" says Prince S., his eyes widening with fear. "Their stupor dwindles!"

"Those are the real Couriers!" you say, looking up at him.

"Traitor!" Ember shouts as—*FOOM!*—a white-hot fireball barrels toward you. You dodge, but it grazes the paper you hold. You can't believe Ember would throw fireballs in here. With the amount of paper in this room, you all could burn to a crisp. Not to mention all the Originals. Evil or not, why would she endanger stories?

Fire curls around the edges of the page. You drop it

and throw your body down on it, rolling back and forth to smother the flames. No sooner do you roll onto your back than your eyes fill with the terrifying sight of the giant dung beetle towering over you. Fire beneath you and insectoid death from above—needless to say, not an ideal position to find yourself in.

"It doesn't have to be this way," the duplicate Larry says as he reaches down and hooks his spiky legs into you. You feel the heat from the fireball dying against your fabulous evening wear. Guess you will only be wearing this outfit once. The dung beetle hoists you off the ground and brings you up to his face. "Don't make me hurt you," he says. If you thought friendly Larry was scary, Scary Larry is a thousand times scarier. You know that his industrial-strength arms could easily break you in half. Though you struggle against his grip with all your might, it makes no difference.

At your sudden height in the dung beetle's pretarsi, you see your friends onstage. They shake their limbs groggily, as if they just woke up from a deep sleep—all but Manteau, who watches, looking rather forlorn, from inside a duplicate trap to the one you wrote for the other Manteau.[82]

---

82 Maybe you should have been more specific about which Manteau you meant to trap, seeing as how you unintentionally trapped both. But give yourself a break, you can't think of everything.

"Just cooperate with us," he says. *Cooperate with them?* As in help them imprison the real Couriers? How could you do that? Though they may look exactly the same, these new Couriers seem totally different to you. They'll stop at nothing to protect the device, even if it means destroying Originals. Or you.

"No way!" you say. "My real friends would never do this!"

"In that case," Scary Larry says, "I'm going to have to treat you like you treated the device."

Scary Larry raises you above his head. You remember smashing your device on the floor of the GPS. Looks like that's what he has planned for you. He rears back—

CLINK! CLINK! You look down and see Prince S. thrusting his sword against Scary Larry's thick beetle armor. The S. Word finds its way between the interlocking plates of the dung beetle's exoskeleton and jabs him. Scary Larry lurches in pain, dropping you into the heart of a massive paper pile. Evil Ember grabs hold of Prince S.'s blade. Its silver color turns a blazing red.

"AGGH!" Prince S. cries, dropping his steaming sword on the floor and reigniting the singed paper that you just put out.

"I don't like it when you use the S. Word," Evil Ember snipes at the captain as he blows on his hands in a vain attempt to cool them down.

The ninja turns to you, flames burning in her eyes. "Looks like you're in the hot seat now," she says. When you're up to your neck in kindling, the last thing you want to hear is a tiny pyromaniac[83] cracking fire jokes. She cups her little hands and a swirling ball of fire forms between her palms.

BLAM!

A rainbolt barrels into the ninja, knocking her to the ground. You look up. Alicole hovers near the ceiling of the dining hall, her crossbow still pointed at Evil Ember.

"You're awake!" you shout. You look over to the stage and see your Courier comrades making their way to your aid. The trap crumbles to ash around Manteau as the page you wrote it on disintegrates. The evil Manteau is free, too, but from the looks of it,

83 Someone who suffers from an uncontrollable urge to set things on fire. A dangerous friend, but useful at a cookout.

he knocked himself out when he smashed into the side of your trap. You can hear him snoring from here.[84] Now that they've recovered, you and your friends outnumber the duplicates four to one. You can almost taste victory.

"Nova!" Prince S. shouts. "What fresh treachery is this?"

In the doorway to the dining hall stands the slim figure of the chamalien's duplicate, holding your device in one of her four hands. Guess you shouldn't have left it on the ship. You rip your S. Word from its sheath and toss it to Prince S.

"Prince S.!" you shout as he catches the sword. "Stop her!"

Too late. Using her shortest arm, she lifts your device to her mouth and says, "Duplicates, attack!"

You feel a rumble. It grows to a quake that shakes the walls of the dining hall, and a flood of scribbles, squiggles, and sketches spews into the room. Baron Terrain's and Banjoe's doubles charge in along with them. You bury your head in the paper pile to take cover. The sounds of rainbolts, bullets, and fireballs explode all around you. Above the fray, you hear the two Banjoes squaring off:

"Ain't no quicker picker than me!" "Ain't no quicker

---

84 He snores just like the real Manteau. Don't tell anyone.

picker than me!" they both say, and unleash a musical onslaught at each other. As if one Banjoe wasn't hard enough on the ears, now the entire room has to endure dueling Banjoes:

"Now I don't want to bicker,
But I'm the quicker picker!"

> *"Yer a mosey-dozin' poseur,*
> *You think that I'd suppose yer*
> *Some finger-pickin' slicker*
> *When I'm the quicker picker?"*

"Yer just a common booger flicker,
You ain't no quicker picker!"

> *"Don't go makin' people sicker*
> *Claimin' you're the quicker picker!"*

You dig yourself deeper down, trying to muffle the competing twangs. Titles of Originals brush past your eyes and an idea strikes you. Somewhere in the dining hall lies the Original of your device. If you can find it and erase it, or destroy it, the duplicates will cease to exist.

Papers shift next to your head. You brace yourself for whatever Doodling double has found you. But instead of a sketchy scribble, you see two little black eyes peering at you from a furry face.

"Manteau!" you whisper.

"*Allô!*" Manteau says in his friendly French accent. "I saw you bravely hide in here and I thought I would courageously join you. I don't want to get too close to any of those Doodlings. It seems like there are twice as many as there were before!"

"It's because of the device!" you say. "We have to find the device's Original and destroy it."

"I told you zat device was trouble!" he says, already exasperated with you. "And now we have to do more erasing?!"

"I don't know, maybe I can edit it so I can turn it off or something. But we have to find it!"

"All right, all right." He sighs. "Let's see . . ." Manteau grabs a page by your shoulder and reads the title. "Here it is!"

"No way!" you say. "You found it?"

"*Zee Little Cheese Dancer!*" he says. "I thought I'd never see it again."

"Manteau!" you shout. "Come on!"

You and the stoat snatch at the pages and scan the titles, but it's no use. There are thousands of Originals in this room.[85] It would take days to find it, and that would be without the onslaught of attacking Doodlings. You almost wish you had let Evil Ember torch the place. But then you think of all the characters who would vanish if that happened. You have to protect them, even if you're not a Courier.

"Help!" Alicole shouts. "There are too many of them!"

Speaking of protecting fictional characters, your friends need you. They face an army of duplicate doodles. Time to even the odds. You take your pencil out and grab the nearest sheet of paper, dreaming up an army of your own.

But before your pencil touches the page, slender fingers wrap around it and yank it out of your grasp. The thieving hand snakes away in a flash. You poke your head out of the safety of your paper igloo. The cold, unfeeling eyes of the duplicate Nova stare down at you from behind her thick glasses. With your pencil in hand, her skin sparkles into a triumphant gold.

"Thank you," she says icily. "Now we can utilize this eraser on the original Original."

---

85 12,802, some say.

Her words floor you. *Erase the original Original?* It goes against everything you know about this world. The duplicate Couriers can't be that bad, can they?

"But why?" you say. "Why would you want to erase the original Original? You'll destroy yourselves and all of Astorya!"

"We do not intend to erase *A Story of Astorya,*" she says. "We will simply improve it."

"Like add more to it?" you say. "You can't! You're not real."

"No," she says.

"Improve it by deleting the extraneous details."

Extraneous details? What is she talking about?

Then the horror of their plan begins to sink in. The copycat Couriers don't care about protecting the Originals, they only care about protecting the copies. And all the copies are stored on your device. That's why Ember's duplicate didn't mind incinerating stories to stop you. If the fake Couriers erase the Couriers from *A Story of Astorya*, the real Couriers will disappear. But the picture of the original Original on your device will remain intact, and so will the fake Couriers.

"Precisely," the bogus Nova says, reading your thoughts.

You try to steady your nerves. They don't have the story. They haven't won yet. "You'd have to find it first," you say. "And I'll never tell you where it is."

"You already did," she says. "On board the ship. I read it in your brain waves."

NO! She was there the whole time. Camouflaged. And the fake Couriers asked you all those questions about where you hid the story. You feel monumentally stupid. The first time you met the real Nova, she was invisible in the GPS! *How could I forget?!*

"That I do not know," Bogus Nova responds to your thought.

"Even if you do know where it is," you say, "you won't be able to get it. I made sure of that."

"Alicole has already acquired it," Bogus Nova says.

"You're lying," you say.

"Incorrect. I have been monitoring her thoughts. She located the tear outside New Spielburg and she just obtained the receptacle you wrote in the middle of the *MIDDLE*."

You thought you had been so clever to erase the word bridges leading to the story, but your ingenious plan had one gaping hole: fictional characters that can fly. And since the duplicate Alicole is technically a Courier, she can open the box.

"You should be pleased," Bogus Nova says. "You improved upon our design. The device allows us to communicate with each other instantaneously. Is this not what you intended?"

You collapse inside. They have the original Original. They have your pencil. They have your eraser. They've beaten you.

And it's all your fault. You made the device. You made the copy.

You can't win. What's the use in fighting?

"You are wise to contemplate surrender," Bogus Nova says. "If you concede defeat, you will not be harmed.

We can devise a plan to return you to your world." She stashes your pencil in her jumpsuit and brings the device up to her mouth. "Your device is listening. You only have to say the word, and all this violence will cease. Then you will have not only saved Astorya again, but improved it. Especially once we remove the redundant Couriers."

"No!" you scream. "You can't do that! You can't just get rid of the real Couriers!"

"Why not?" she asks, looking genuinely perplexed.

"I'll tell you why not!" Manteau yells. He darts past you and runs up the false chamalien's leg.

"Duplicates—" she says into your device. But before she can finish her sentence, the stoat chomps down on her hand with his razor-sharp teeth. "Ow," she yelps, her skin turning red as a pimple. The device falls to the floor.

"Run!" Manteau shouts, scurrying around on Bogus Nova's torso, dodging her many swatting hands. "Take zee device!"

You grab the device and scramble to your feet.

"Stop the real human!" Bogus Nova cries.

Innumerable Doodling doubles barricade the door to the dining hall, while what seems like even more Doodling doubles rush at you from all sides. As your friends swoop in to stem the enemy tide, the maddening racket of the

Banjoes grows louder. You'll never make it through the door with all those duplicates blocking it. But then you remember another way out of this room. Darting around raging battles and mounds of stories with a trail of Doodling duplicates on your tail, you bolt for the stage and the secret slide passage.

As you run past the dining table, the mountainous form of Baron Terrain's double blocks your path. "Sorry, kid," he says, training his six-shooter on you. "It's over." You grab a sticky bun off the table and toss it into the air. Unable to resist, he lunges after it and catches it in his teeth. *Nom-nom-nom!* While he's consumed with consuming, you race past him and dive into a pile of Originals on the stage.

Frantically, you plow on toward where you remember emerging from the secret passage. Pages swish as Doodling copies plunge into the paper pile after you. An ampersand[86] throws itself around your neck. Little asterisks poke you in the face. Googly eyes burrow into your armpits. Squiggles wrap around your legs, pinning them together. You bat at yourself like a trespasser on a mosquito farm. Though only a few yards stand between

---

86 One of those "&" symbols, although at the moment, you may feel more like #*%@!

yourself and the slide, the Doodling doubles have you in their sketchy clutches.

"Off with you, counterfeits!" you hear Prince S. command. Though you can't see him with asterisks in your eyes, Prince S. bounds onto the stage, wielding both S. Words. With a quickness, he knocks the doodle doubles off your body with one sword and skewers them with the other, making one of the S. Words into an impressive Doodling-duplicate shish kebab.

Free at last, you scramble toward the passageway. *FOOM!* A fireball barrels into you with such force that it knocks you into a pile of stories. Evil Ember must have recovered from Alicole's rainbolt. Flailing wildly, you bat the fireball away from you. It leaves a burning trail across your already-singed evening wear and ignites the paper pile. As you try to beat down the flames curling up along your body, an inferno of Originals blazes around you.

An iridescent blur plows into you. Smashed up against a hard exoskeleton and held there by spiky legs, you find yourself in the violent embrace of the dung beetle. Scary Larry has you in his unshakable grip. You squirm uselessly as he rolls you over and over on the ground, fearing the squeeze that you know is coming.

But instead of a squeeze, you feel his arms unfold.

"Go!" he says, releasing you. "I'll take care of the fire!"

It's the real Larry! He launches himself onto the flames as you lunge into the passageway.

CHAPTER SEVENTEEN

The sounds of battle and banjos fade as the slide carries you up a steep incline. You pat yourself down in the darkness, trying to ensure Larry's spiky stop-drop-and-roll maneuver fully extinguished Evil Ember's fireball.

After a sharp turn, the slide levels out and you see the late-day rays of the Astoryan sun spilling through the enormous glass wall. Outside sits the Hole that you passed on the way to the Other Side. You remember Manteau's umbrella and how the top half of it completely vanished when you put it in the Hole. Come to think of it, that's the only time you've ever seen a fictional object permanently affected by anything other than erasure.

That's it, you think. *I'll throw it in the Hole.* If the device disappears from Astorya, so will the picture of the original Original, and so will all the copies. If you can somehow escape from the castle unnoticed and race to the Hole, you may just have a chance. Nova may be listening to your thoughts, but you've got the device, so she can't issue any commands into it and share your plan with all of copykind instantly. *Do you hear that, Nova?* you think. *I figured out how to beat you!*

The slide winds back through the entrails of the castle and takes you to the gym. You tumble out of the opening in the wall onto the squeaky floor. Immediately, something bites you on your shoulder. "OW!" you cry as you swat at it. Swirls and scribbles trickle out of the secret passage behind you. The thing biting your shoulder sinks its teeth into your hand. You pull your hand back and see a fang-toothed smiley face clamping down on it. It laugh-growls as you try to shake it off. These Doodling duplicates may look harmless, but enough of them together could easily finish you off.

The clattering of sticks echoes through the room. Sphincter and the stick figures fight with their stick twins in two neat rows. Each one has ripped off an arm and fences with it like an épée.[87]

Sphincter looks over at you and yells, "Help the Word Champion!" Half the stick figures rush over to you, and the other half rush after them. You'll just have to hope that the ones in front are the real ones.

You jab your fingers into the smiley face's eyes. "That hurts!" he says joyfully, releasing his fangs from your hand. You grab him by the sides of his head.

"Look out!" you call to your stick figure allies. They lunge out of the way just as you granny-style bowl the smiley face toward the oncoming stick figure doubles. Strike! The stick figure copies go flying and you dash out of the room.

Sphincter and his comrades follow quick on your heels. "What's the plan, Word Champion?" he says.

"I have to get this device to the Hole outside!" you say.

As soon as the words leave your lips, you wish you could shove them back in. But it's too late. Your device heard you. A new rumble of impending doubles tells you that your plan is no longer a secret.

You and the stick figures run through the hall and turn a corner. A mob of duplicates awaits at the end of the hallway. It didn't take long for them to find you. Even with

---

87 If Manteau were here, he could tell you that this is a French word for a dueling sword. You can discuss it with him later, assuming you survive.

your ten stick fighters, you wouldn't stand a chance against the sheer volume of doodle doubles surging toward you.

After two weeks of lounging around this castle, you know it pretty well. And you recognize this hallway. It's the one with the lab. Maybe science will save your life.

You duck into the doorway and grab one of the exploding beakers off the shelf. Hoping it doesn't go off in your hand, you dash back out to the hallway and hurl it at the oncoming duplicates. *KAPOWW!!!* The blast throws them high into the air. "Come on!" you shout to the stick figures and charge ahead, dodging the hail of pound signs and check marks.

Another mass of doodle doubles appears around the corner and stampedes toward you. "In here!" you say, sidestepping into the room you share with Manteau. The stick figures file in after you, and you slam the door shut. If only you had an extra pencil in here, you could write yourself something to fend off this angry horde of jots, dashes, and warring peace signs. The door shakes as the Doodling doubles try to break it down. You're out of options. The only way out of this room is the window. But you wouldn't survive the fall. Why did you have to write this place to be so tall and majestic?

"I need to get to the Hole," you tell Sphincter. "Any ideas?"

"Say no more, Word Champion!" he says and rushes to the open window. The other stick figures all line up and leap out the window one by one. Ritual suicide doesn't quite fit their character, so you stick your head out the window and look down. To your astonishment, you see that they have formed a stick figure ladder[88] down the wall of the castle by locking each one's hands around the next one's ankles. You clamber out the window just as the doubles break down the door.

You climb down the ladder as quickly as you can, but when you reach the last stick figure, your feet dangle. You look down. Still quite a ways to go. But when you look up and see the doubles emerge from the window, you decide to take your chances with gravity. You let go of the last stick figure and drop the rest of the way.

The unforgiving ground of the Margins punishes your body when you meet it. Your ankle gets the worst of it, but there's a lot worse to come if you don't move fast. You hobble-run toward the Hole. Over your shoulder, you glimpse rivers of Doodling doubles pouring out of the castle from every door and window. What sounds like an

---

88 We know. They don't look like this anymore. Feel free to make the appropriate changes (in case you need a break from running for your life).

earthquake booms behind you. You turn and see in the distance a tsunami of copies washing over the mountains, heading your way. Looks like your device has sent every duplicate in Astorya to stop you.

Cringing with pain, you limp-sprint onward. At least the land is flat; you don't think you could handle running uphill right now. The Doodling doubles tickle your heels. They've almost caught up to you. The Hole looks so close, and yet you never seem to get there. Exhaustion drags on your every muscle. Or maybe that's the duplicates grabbing you. You falter and stagger, but keep going. More duplicates glom on to your ankles, especially the hurt one. You'll never make it. Your only hope is to throw the device.

You wind up like a quarterback about to launch the final throw of the game. With the little strength you have left, you hurl the device at the Hole. But the device never leaves your fingers.

You look in horror to see that a scribble has wrapped itself around your hand, tying the device to it. You attempt to pry it off, but more Doodling doubles coil around your fingers, transforming both your hands into useless tangled balls.

You stumble as more and more duplicates pile onto you. You wonder if their plan is to suffocate you. Whether they planned it or not, it's working. You can hardly breathe as you press forward. Just before the tic-tac-toes blot out your vision completely, you see the Hole gaping just a few feet in front of you. *I'm almost there. I'm going to make it. I'm going to make it!*

The duplicates tie your legs together. You fall flat on your face, ejecting the rest of your breath out of your lungs.

I'm not going to make it.

Lying there only inches from victory, you feel like a helpless heap of almost. Almost made it. Almost righted your wrong. Almost saved the day.

As if the weight of your defeat wasn't crushing enough, copies continue to pile on top of you, cementing you into the ground. At this rate, your bones will give up long before these doubles do. Eventually, every duplicate in Astorya will throw itself on top of what Evil Ember will turn into your funeral pyre.[89]

It's not too late, you think. You can still save yourself. Bogus Nova said you wouldn't be harmed, and they would even figure out a way to get you home. *All I have to do is tell the device I'm giving up.* If you're going to lose anyway,

---

89 A heap made for burning a corpse. Although in this case, the pyre is going to make you into a corpse.

what's the use in dying? *I either lose and die, or I lose and live.*

The tone of those thoughts strikes you as familiar—your red voice. You thought you had left it behind on the Other Side, but it's still with you. It wants you to survive. To give in. To let the copies win.

But if you survive, it means your friends don't.

Who cares? They're fictional, remember?

They may be fictional, but they are your real friends. If you betray them, what does that make you?

Someone you don't want to be. Someone you don't like. Someone you couldn't face in the mirror.

There will be no looking in any mirror if I don't give up now. I'll be crushed at the bottom of this pile. Death by doubles. And the Couriers will survive—at least their copies will. But there's no copy of me. I have to save myself.

Your red voice may be right, but you still feel it's wrong. You can't bring yourself to give in to your device. You heave out one final breath.

So this is the way you end—not as the hero, but as the failure.

Perhaps it serves you right for not listening to your friends. But then you remember that this punishment will destroy them, too. It will destroy Astorya as you know it.

In fact, the duplicate Couriers could be erasing them right now.

No! I can't let them down! your most redless voice screams in your head. You didn't come all this way to give up now. That's not who you are. You may not know your name. Or your address. But those are just details. Who you are is much more than that. It doesn't have to be lose-and-die or lose-and-live. You can still win. If you can just reach the Hole. It can't be far now.

New strength rises from deep inside you. Enough strength to wriggle your body forward. *I did it! I moved! I can make it. I will make it!* Like a worm, you inch closer to the Hole.

But what do I do when I get to it? The doubles won't let you let go of the device. You'll have to stick your hand in there. And that means—

You will lose your hand.

The thought makes you shudder. But it's a small price to pay when you consider what hangs in the balance.

Sticking your arm out in front of you, you feel for where the land drops away into that inky nothingness.

The Hole! You found it! You made it! Tears of relief drop onto the doubles covering your face.

With one last heave, you raise your duplicate-encrusted

hand. You can still feel the device firmly roped against your palm. You take a deep breath, say goodbye to your hand, and lower it into the Hole.

Before your heart can even complete its beat, the duplicates disappear. Your body falls a couple of inches, since the duplicates who were underneath you are no more.

You roll over and sit up, checking the horizon. No approaching army of duplicate Astoryans comes to destroy you.

Laughter gushes out of you. You did it! You got rid of the copies!

And.

Your hand.

Of course, it had to be your writing hand.

It's gone. Like Manteau's umbrella, there's no sign of damage. No bones, no blood, just a nub at the end of your wrist where your hand used to live.

CHAPTER EIGHTEEN

You don't know how long you've been crying when your
friends find you. It could have been two minutes or
two hours. But seeing them all happily tromping your way
grants you a momentary reprieve from your tears. At least
they all made it in one piece.

"You did it!" Manteau cheers from atop Larry's shell. "Zat
fake Manteau wiz his borrowed dance moves is no more!"

"But why is your face so stricken with sorrow, friend?"
asks Prince S. "Do you not feel the wings of victory lifting
you on high?"

"It's just battle exhaustion," says Alicole. "You've had an
epic day."

"Oh no," Nova says, turning amber with alarm.

"Something irreparable has occurred."

"Right, we know, zee doubles are gone for good!" Manteau says, sliding down Larry's shell and bounding over to you. "So, are you going to keep us all in suspense forever? How did you do it? I know you did not erase zee device's Original."

"No," you say. "I mean, yeah, the doubles are gone, but Nova's right. I lost something."

"Yes," Alicole says, trotting over to you. "I picked up your pencil for you. I saw it fall from the false Nova when she disappeared with the others." She holds out your pencil to you.

When you start to reach for it with your nonexistent hand, a new barrage of tears tumbles out of your eyes.

"It's okay, I cry sometimes, too," Larry offers.

You lift your stump for all your friends to see. They gasp. No one can wrench their eyes away from your handlessness.

"I lost my hand," you say.

"I can see zat!" Manteau cries. "But what did you do zat for?"

"I had to. I stuck it in the Hole."

"Zee Hole?! Zee Hole right here zat swallows everything it touches?! Why would you do zat? How could you forget what happened to my umbrella?"

"The doubles knew that I was going to throw the device in the Hole. So they tied it to my hand."

"Whoa," Ember says. "So you stuck your hand in that Hole to get rid of the device?"

"Yeah," you say. Gaping at that infinite inkiness beside you, you can hardly believe it yourself.

"Awesome." The little fire ninja nods at you. "Master Tanuki would be proud." The fire glowing warmly in her eyes tells you that she has forgiven you. And you only had to lose your hand. Not quite a fair trade, but such is the way of the ninja.

Prince S. helps you to your feet. "Friend," he says. "We have seen many battles, but we bear no scars. You have sacrificed yourself in a way that no fictional character ever could. Astorya is forever in your debt."

"Does it hurt?" asks Larry.

"No," you say. "It's just gone."

"Wear your wound with pride," says Alicole. "It is a testament to your bravery."

With your forearm, you try to wipe away your tears, but only manage to smear snot across your cheeks. Not your proudest moment. You hope Alicole doesn't notice as you take the pencil from her with your remaining hand.

"Guess you'll have to learn how to write with your other hand," Ember says.

You laugh as a fresh avalanche of tears falls from your eyes.

"Theoretically," Nova says, "you could write yourself a fictional hand."

"Really?" You sniffle. You hadn't thought of that. It's nice to have a superintelligent being on your side. Much nicer than having her as an enemy. Hope stanches your tears.

"Oooh," Ember says, getting excited. "You can make it so your hand can throw fireballs."

"Or shoot rainbolts," Alicole says.

"I recommend the addition of a few more fingers," Nova suggests. "Highly useful."

"Make some of the fingers pretarsi," Larry adds. "You'll be able to crawl up walls. Comes in handy." He flinches, realizing his faux pas.[90] "Oh! Sorry. I didn't mean . . . sorry."

"It's okay," you say to Larry, offering him a smile.

"Make it furry," Manteau says, "wiz claws, so you can scratch your enemies and those hard-to-reach places. Like my back."

If you took all these suggestions, you would create the

---

90 An embarrassing or tactless remark. Not to be confused with "faux paw," which is what you're currently contemplating.

most ludicrously fantastical, preposterously powerful, and generally freakish hand of all time. But making it that way would involve a lot of writing.

"It was my writing hand," you say. "It'll take me forever to write anything."

"You don't know till you try," Larry says, sounding upbeat. "Maybe it won't be so bad."

Using your good hand (the one that didn't vanish into a mysterious void), you dig into your vest for a fresh piece of paper and pull out—

The device!

"No! No! No!" you say, hurling it into the Hole. You don't know how it possibly got back in there after everything you went through to get rid of it, but you don't want to waste another second pondering it before the doubles reappear.

"What was zat?" Manteau shrieks.

"Was that the device?" asks Larry.

"I . . . I don't understand. I stuck the device and my hand in the Hole and all the doubles disappeared. It happened. I mean, look at my hand! But then, just now, you saw that, right? I went to get some paper and—"

You reach back into your vest. The device! You pull out another device and stare at it. It stares back at you as if you had never put it in the Hole. Either time.

"What's happening?!" you say, feeling like your brain might have a heart attack. "I can't get rid of it!"

Everyone crowds around to get a look at the eternal reoccurrence of your device.

"Does that mean the duplicates are coming back?" Larry asks, his voice quivering with worry. "I really didn't like how mean the other me was."

"We'll be ready for them this time." Alicole whips her crossbow out of its holster.

"Wait!" you say. "They might not be coming back."

"They had enough, eh?" Manteau puffs up his tiny furry chest. "I must say they were good, but not as good-looking."

"Just hold on." You place the device on the ground, searching for the image of the original Original. But no images appear. No pictures of your friends. It's like it was just after you wrote it, brand-new. "The Original of this thing is still in the dining hall, right?"

"Presumably," Nova responds. "Although approximately seven hundred thirty-two stories received varying degrees of fire damage."

"It wasn't me," grumbles Ember. "Well, it was me, but not me me, it was the bad me. You know what I mean."

"So, will you keep getting a new device no matter how many times you throw it in the Hole?" Larry asks.

"Let's see," you say, tossing it into the Hole again. You reach into your vest and pull out yet another device.

"As you have demonstrated," Nova says, "we can now assume that the device will continue to reconstitute itself as long as its Original remains in our world. The iteration of your device that contained the image of the original Original, however, has been removed from this dimension, and therefore, so have the duplicates."

"So this hole leads to another dimension?" you ask.

"That is a viable hypothesis," she says. "But we cannot say for certain. In any case, it may be advisable to stop throwing your device inside."

Three different copies of your device drift somewhere out there in the multiverse, and one of them has your hand attached to it. But your hand is real, and the device is fictional (not to mention all those Doodling doubles wrapped around it). Can fictional objects exist outside of Astorya? Is there a chance you may be reunited with your hand someday?

"Alternatively," Nova says, "this Hole may be a singularity that completely annihilates whatever touches it."

So much for your space-hand reunion.

"Zee important thing," says Manteau, "is zat zee dastardly doubles are gone for good. And zee best part is zat you got rid of them wizout erasing anything!"

"Manteau," you say.

"What? Zat is good, *non*?"

"I lost my hand!"

"Well, at least you didn't have to erase anything," he mutters.

You shake your head at the little stoat.

"If only I had had the chance to face my double," says Alicole, still cradling her crossbow in her arms. "I wonder why she fled. That is not like me."

"She did not flee," Manteau says. "Zee fake Couriers had a depraved plan to erase us real Couriers from zee original Original! She was retrieving it."

"Erase us?" Alicole huffs.

Nova's skin breaks out in pink polka dots of surprise.

"They really were evil," says Ember.

"But how come?" Larry asks. "Shouldn't they be just like us?"

"They were," you say. Your friends look at you, baffled.

"*Mais non!*" protests Manteau. "We are not evil! We are good!"

"Yes," you say, "you are. Because you don't listen to your red voices."

"Red voices?" asks Larry.

"It's the voice of your worst self," you say. "On the Other Side, it gets louder and harder to ignore. But now I see that the Other Side doesn't give it to you. We all have one. So they were just like you. Only they listened to their red voices. And it told them to obey the device."

"I would never obey zat device!" says Manteau.

"Me neither!" says Ember.

"Nor I," says Alicole.

"Couriers," Prince S. says with a severity that silences them, "our friend here speaks the truth. Good and evil are but twins housed beneath the selfsame roof. Had you been to the Other Side, you would understand." He turns to you. "But how did the false Couriers divine the location of . . . of . . . you know . . ."

"The original Original?" asks Larry.

"That's it!" he says.

"The other Nova," you say. "When we were on the GPS, I thought of where I hid it. I didn't know she was there, reading my thoughts. It was my fault. And after everything—" Thoughts of monsters and lava and cockroaches catch your tongue. The red voice, the red eyes, teetering over the endless abyss, you endured so much to find the perfect spot to hide the original Original. But it didn't stay hidden more than an hour. If you hadn't made a copy of Astorya, there would be no false Couriers to trick you into revealing its location. And if the false Alicole already found it and then disappeared on her way back to Castle Doodling when you stuck the device in the Hole, the original Original must have fallen to the ground somewhere between New Spielburg and here. It could be anywhere. The weight of your failure drags you down like an anchor dropped into a bottomless sea. Your head slumps and you look at your stump. "It was all for nothing."

"Correction," Nova says. "The weakness of your previous hiding spot was that you knew its location, as exploited so adeptly by my duplicate. But now, because you created and removed the duplicates, no one knows its location."

"That would mean," says Alicole, "the original Original is now the most secure it has ever been."

"Affirmative," Nova continues. "Especially considering the receptacle you wrote for it, making it impossible for anyone but yourself or a Courier to access it. If I didn't know your thoughts, I would have assumed this was your plan from the start."

"Brilliant!" Ember says. "If none of us know its location,

the next Rulette can't brain-squeeze any of us to find out where it is."

Prince S. shudders. "That vile queen abused my sorry dome beyond all . . . all . . . agh! Why do my words flee? Like common cowards they—"

"Well," Manteau interrupts, "at least we know zat will never happen again. And all zee copies are gone." He beams at you. "You saved zee day once more!"

"Wait," says Larry. "How come not everyone had copies?"

"Everyone did," you say. "I mean, except me. Oh, and Prince S."

"But isn't he part of the original Original?" Larry asks. No one responds, but everyone looks perplexed. You get the feeling that none of these characters have ever read the story that makes them exist.

Manteau's eyes crease in agitation. "Well?" he says. "You tell us. You memorized it, didn't you?"

"Um . . . ," you stall. You didn't memorize it, but you read it, and you can't remember Prince S.'s character description. Or if he even had one. "I don't know," you say.

"What do you mean you don't know?!" Manteau shouts. "You forgot it already?"

"This is why I made the device in the first place!" you shout back at him. "So I wouldn't have to memorize it!"

"So you didn't memorize it! I knew it!" Manteau throws up his paws in frustration.

Well, it's too late to check now. The picture you took of it has been banished from your current dimension, and the original Original itself lies somewhere in the great unknown. Of course, you, the one reading this book, can check whether Prince S. appears in the original Original by turning to the back of *Mightier Than the Sword*. But that's not going to help you, the one in Astorya.

"Maybe he's part of another story," Ember says.

"If he were part of any story," Nova says, "he would have an Original, and therefore he would also have had a double."

"So what are you saying?" you ask.

"Lack of duplication suggests that Prince S. has no Original," Nova says.

"But he has to," you say. "Right? Isn't that how it works? How else would he be here?" For a moment, you think the chamalien has come to the wrong conclusion. It's too bad Prince S. can't remember who he is. He might be able to give you some sort of clue—

Wait, you think. *Prince S. can't remember who he is. I can't remember who I am.*

You turn to Prince S. "We can't remember who we are.

And we were the only ones without copies."

"Yes, 'tis curious . . . ," Prince S. replies.

"So, maybe . . ." You pause, realizing how preposterous what you are about to suggest sounds. ". . . maybe you're real. Just like me."

"Zat's impossible!" says Manteau. "Prince S. has been our *capitaine* since zee beginning. And zat was thousands of years ago. And, as you told me, people don't live zat long!"

"The distinction between past, present, and future is only a stubbornly persistent illusion,"[91] says Nova. "The relative age of a human being on Earth is irrelevant here."

"So, he could be real!" you say.

"Nay!" Prince S. cries. "I know not why I had no double, but Manteau is in the right. I have always called Astorya my home. And I have always led the Couriers, century after century, and faced foes so fierce that had I been real, I would not have survived to tell the tale. So it follows that I must be fictional."

"I know one way to find out," you say, handing Prince S. your real-world pencil and a piece of paper (one at a time—missing a hand really slows you down). "Write something. If you're fictional, nothing will happen."

---

91 She's right. Just ask Einstein.

"But me?" Prince S. laughs uncomfortably. "My words never fail to fail me! A great writer I am not."

"You don't have to write," you say. "You can draw something."

"But whatever shall I draw?" he asks.

"It doesn't matter," you say. "It could be anything."

Prince S. furrows his brow and bores his eyes into the page.

"Larry?" he calls out. "May I use your carapace?"

"Sure thing, Captain." Larry scuttles over and hunkers down next to him.

Prince S. spreads the page out on Larry's shell, licks his lips, and lifts your pencil high above his head. You wonder if he's going to throw it at the page like a dart. He wiggles his hips and takes a noisy breath in through his nostrils. As he exhales, he slowly brings the pencil to the paper and scribbles something quickly.

"There. You see! I am fictional after all!" he pronounces.

"But, Captain," Alicole says. "Look!"

A hapless-looking doodle hangs in the air. Prince S. holds the paper up and compares it to the object that just appeared. You and your friends huddle behind him to get a better look. It's a perfect match.

"Dear Heavens," Prince S. says.

"No way," Ember says.

"Whoa," Larry says.

"Captain?" Alicole says. For the first time you can remember, the mighty Pegataur sounds afraid.

"*Sacrebleu!*" whispers Manteau.

"Can it be?" Prince S. asks. "Am I . . . real?"

"The evidence would suggest it," says Nova.

"You're really real!" you say in amazement. "Just like me."

"But, then, all this time, I could have been . . . killed?" Prince S. faints, falling backward into Larry's spiky arms.

You and your friends stare at one another in wonderment.

"Are you thinking what I am thinking?" Manteau asks.

"No," Nova replies, reading his thoughts.

"Maybe," Manteau says, his expression growing very serious, "I am a real human being, too!"

"I told you no one was thinking that," Nova says.

Manteau shrugs.

Your mind floods with questions. *Who is Prince S.? How did he get here? When did he get here? Do we know each other back on Earth? What happens to the Couriers if he wants to go back? Who will be their captain? Does he know how to get back? If he does, why hasn't he gone*

home already? What if he doesn't? Are we both stuck here?
Will my memory get just as bad as his the longer I stay?
Can I really live here for thousands of years? Will everyone
I know on Earth be long gone by the time I get home? Will I
ever find out who I really am?

"Are you going to faint, too?" Larry asks you. "Because if
you are, I'll put the captain down."

"No," you say. "I'm okay. But . . ." You struggle to form
your questions into words. "How?"

"I must admit," Nova says, flushing purple with
embarrassment, "I have no explanation."

"First time for everything," Ember says.

"I suggest," says Manteau, "we discuss it all over dinner."

The stoat makes a good point. You can't unlock the
secrets of the universe on an empty stomach. Thankfully,
you wrote an amazing castle, complete with magical
endless food, back when you could write freely. You take
a step and remember that you seriously damaged your
ankle. Seeing you wince in pain, Alicole trots over and
swings you up onto her back.

Manteau scurries up her flank and onto your shoulder.
With you on the Pegataur's back, and Prince S. held in the
giant dung beetle's spiky arms, your party trudges back to
Castle Doodling. You smile at your friends. Even though

you probably broke your ankle. Even though you lost your writing hand. Even though you will have to log untold hours practicing to get your other one up to speed. You have your friends back. And now, you also have a fellow real human being.

So, give yourself a hand.[92] You saved Astorya once again.

THE END

---

92 Sorry, we couldn't resist.

*A*PPENDIX

Not Enough French to Speak French,
but Enough to Sound Like Maybe
You Know How

A Word About Words

Crossworld Clues

Not Enough French to Speak French, but Enough to Sound Like Maybe You Know How

Here are some of the words Manteau uses throughout the book. Words in **bold** are the real French words. The rest are just our attempt to capture Manteau's attempt to speak English.

Absolument—absolutely

Adieu—literally "to God," but people almost always mean it to be a more casual, less permanent "goodbye"

Allô—a French version of the English "hello," not to be confused with "aloe," a plant that can soothe the pain of a sunburn (*un coup de soleil* in French)

Bon—good (if you say it twice, *bonbon*, someone might give you some candy)

Bon appétit—literally "good appetite," but in practice, "enjoy the food"

Bonne chance—"good luck," similar to the English "break a leg" (which is a strange way to wish someone good luck, since breaking one's leg is generally considered bad luck)

Capitaine—captain

C'est bon—"it's good," or even just "it's okay"

C'est magnifique!—"it's beautiful!" or "it's wonderful!" but never "it's okay!"

Exactement!—"exactly!," "precisely!," or "quite right!"

Incroyable!—"incredible!," "unbelievable!," or "amazing!"

Je ne sais pas—"I don't know" (that's what it means, we're not trying to get out of defining it)

Mais non—of course not

Non—no

On y va—let's go

Oui—yes

Peut-être—"perhaps" or "maybe"

Quelle horreur—"how awful" or "what a nightmare"

Sacrebleu—a mild, polite curse (similar to "egads," "holy moly," or "dagnabbit")

Un moment—a moment (as in "gimme a sec," rather than "we shared 'a moment'")

Végétation—vegetation (just like it looks without the accents)

Vraiment—"truly," "honestly," or "really"

Wiz—with

Zat—that

Zee—the

Zut alors—a mild, polite curse (we already covered this above with *sacrebleu*, dagnabbit!)

A Word About Words

Throughout this book, you'll need to fill in the blanks with your own words. Below are some helpful definitions for those moments when your pencil and your wits are all you've got to save the rest of you.

Adjective—a word that describes a noun. *Happy, sad, Kafka-esque,* etc.

Adverb—a word that describes a verb. "The giant *slowly* walked up to the doughnut shop." "The doughnuts *quickly* ran away."

Article of clothing—anything you can wear. *T-shirt, tuxedo, tuxedo T-shirt,* etc.

Body part—if it's part of a body, it's a body part. *Hand, foot, tail,* etc.

Collective noun—a noun that refers to a group of individuals. *Bunch, gang, murder* (that last one only applies to crows), etc.

Color—one band, or a mixture of bands, on the spectrum of visible light your eye perceives. *Red, yellow, blue, raw umber, burnt sienna,* etc.

Exclamation—a sudden vocalization that usually expresses pain, anger, surprise, or extreme delight, such as *ouchies!*, *dagnabbit!*, *egads!*, or *yippee!*

Noun—a word that names a person, place, or thing. *Car, pet, carpet*, etc.

Past tense verb—a word used to describe an action that happened in the past. *Came, saw, conquered*, etc.

Place name—anywhere you can be. *Your living room, the moon, Sheboygan*, etc.

Plural noun—a word that names more than one person, place, or thing. *Brothers, bathrooms, bandages*, etc.

Superlative adjective—an adjective that describes the highest degree of comparison. *Biggest, smallest, shortest, tallest*, etc.

Verb—a word that describes an action. *Jump, fall, scream, flail, splatter*, etc.

Verb ending in "-ing"—a word that describes an action happening now. *Sitting, knitting, spitting*, etc.

Verb ending in "s"—a word that describes an action that's happening now. *Tries, flies, cries*, etc.

Crossworld Clues

Fill in the crossworld on page 250 by solving the clues below. We're including the page numbers where the answers can be found in case you get stuck!

Across

1. The emotion you might feel while peering over the precipice of a bottomless pit (page 210)
2. Cruel or devilish in the extreme (page 132)
4. How you might describe a bad apple (page 35)
8. Falsehoods (page 220)
9. Total chaos, mass hysteria, pandemonium, your average night in Monstropolis (page 215)
12. Partner of unusual punishment (page 133)
14. Acceptable or satisfactory. Can also mean sufficiently clothed to see visitors (page 196)
16. The opposite of 8-across (page 25)
18. When you accomplish what you set out to do (page 75)
19. Sort of like 18-across, but even more so (page 117)
24. Not confined, imprisoned, or otherwise encumbered (page 169)

Down

ALANA HARRISON AND DREW CALLANDER

love to crack jokes, talk in funny voices, and read aloud. Imagine their delight to discover that they could combine all these "skills" to write books. In addition to writing books, they've worked as actors, improv comedians, filmmakers, animators, and puppeteers. They spent many years reading and performing kids' original stories, which gave them the idea for Astorya—a world where all the wonderful weirdness that kids imagine could come alive. They hope *Mightier Than the Sword* will inspire readers to harness the power of their own creativity.

At this point in a biography, you usually find out where the author lives. We'd *like* to tell you where Drew and Alana live, but they won't stay put. They used to live in New York, then they moved to Vermont, then back to New York City, then to the west coast of Ireland, then to Ohio, and then to a little city outside of Amsterdam. Who knows? They could be moving to your town next. If they do, come by for a visit. You can watch their phenomenal cat do tricks. But hurry, before they move again.

RYAN ANDREWS lives in the Japanese countryside, with his wife, two kids, and their dog, Lucky. A friendly Kodama or two have been known to take up residence in the giant acorn tree that shades the house. Ryan often works at his drawing desk in the early morning hours, to the sound of rummaging wild boar and badgers, who come from the surrounding forest seeking out shiitake mushrooms and fallen chestnuts.